"You ever  **lon asked quietly**

The question her hair in its ght her face. Dillon und but his hand lingered. He took a thick strand and rubbed it between his fingers.

"I thought I was in love once," she said finally. "He didn't reciprocate—I realized I was wasting my time. But—I wasn't surprised. I know what I am."

Dillon looked surprised. "What are you?"

Rachael dropped her eyes. "I'm not beautiful," she said with a shrug. "I'm plain."

Dillon released the strand of hair and laid his palm against her face, marveling at the smoothness of her skin. "I don't think you're plain, Rachael. You've got the nicest skin I've ever seen on a woman. And your eyes are like Christmas ornaments."

"Mr. McKenzie, you're embarrassing me," she said with a nervous laugh.

"And your hair reminds me of a silky curtain. I'd like to see your hair fanned out on my pillow, Rachael."

She gasped at his words and at the images that filled her mind.

"Does that shock you?"

"Yes, it does." She pulled away from his hand on her cheek. "I think it's time—"

He stepped closer. "If that shocks you, then this is going to blow your mind." He'd barely finished speaking when he captured her in his arms and pressed his mouth to hers. . . .

WHAT ARE *LOVESWEPT* ROMANCES?

They are stories of true romance and touching emotion. We believe those two very important ingredients are constants in our highly sensual and very believable stories in the *LOVESWEPT* line. Our goal is to give you, the reader, stories of consistently high quality that may sometimes make you laugh, sometimes make you cry, but are always fresh and creative and contain many delightful surprises within their pages.

Most romance fans read an enormous number of books. Those they truly love, they keep. Others may be traded with friends and soon forgotten. We hope that each *LOVESWEPT* romance will be a treasure—a "keeper." We will always try to publish

LOVE STORIES YOU'LL NEVER FORGET
BY AUTHORS YOU'LL ALWAYS REMEMBER

The Editors

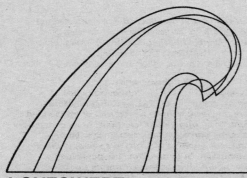

LOVESWEPT® • 494

Charlotte Hughes

The Lady and the Cowboy

 BANTAM BOOKS
NEW YORK • TORONTO • LONDON • SYDNEY • AUCKLAND

THE LADY AND THE COWBOY
A Bantam Book / September 1991

If you would be interested in receiving protective vinyl
covers for your Loveswept books, please write to this address
for information:

Loveswept
Bantam Books
P.O. Box 985
Hicksville, NY 11802

ISBN 0-553-44183-3

Published simultaneously in the United States and Canada

Bantam Books are published by Bantam Books, a division
of Bantam Doubleday Dell Publishing Group, Inc. Its trademark, consisting of the words "Bantam Books" and the
portrayal of a rooster, is Registered in U.S. Patent and
Trademark Office and in other countries. Marca Registrada.
Bantam Books, 666 Fifth Avenue, New York, New York
10103.

PRINTED IN THE UNITED STATES OF AMERICA

OPM 0 9 8 7 6 5 4 3 2 1

*To Sandra, who wouldn't leave me alone
until I wrote a cowboy book for her.
Much love to you and yours.*

Prologue

Dillon McKenzie huddled deeper into his saddle-color down jacket and gazed unseeingly at the toes of his lizard skin boots—the ones he saved for Saturday nights—and prepared to be bored as the bespectacled attorney before him read in a monotone voice the legal document he held.

I, ABLE WESLEY PRATT, do hereby make, publish and declare this as and for my Last Will and Testament . . .

Dillon yawned and wished he were somewhere else.

. . . I direct all of my lawful debts, the expense of my last illness and funeral, and the placing of a marker over my grave to my Executrix . . .

Dillon wondered why he had been summoned to the will reading in the first place. Knowing how frugal Abel Pratt had been, Dillon couldn't imagine what his late employer could have left him that would have amounted to anything. Abel had been buried in his boots, so they were out.

Dillon closed his eyes, sighed tiredly, and wondered where he would go now that Abel was dead. At thirty-three, he had worked just about every ranch from the Texas Panhandle to the Dakotas. He had put down roots at the Lazy Acres seven years ago, and he didn't know if it was because Abel Pratt had been so desperate for help that he'd stayed, or because he'd simply found his niche there. Abel had let him run the ranch as he'd seen fit. He was not a man who liked being ordered around, which probably accounted for the years he'd spent drifting. Abel Pratt hadn't seemed to mind that Dillon rode a motorcycle instead of a horse or that he blew his paycheck playing poker at the Mustang Bar and Grill every Saturday night, stayed out until all hours, and was worthless come Sunday. But now Abel was gone and Dillon was out of a job.

. . . I will, devise and bequeath one half of my estate and ranch to Dillon McKenzie, my trusted foreman of seven years. . . .

Dillon's eyes popped open, and he sat upright in his chair. He was the beneficiary of Abel's will? No, it was a mistake. Abel hadn't even liked him. But then, he told himself, Abel hadn't liked anybody. Of course, if anyone deserved the ranch it was him. He had pulled it out of the red. And he'd personally seen to it that Abel had taken his medicine when he'd become ill, had driven him to town for his doctor's appointments. But half? The will said half.

. . . and the other half to Reverend Rachael Caitland, daughter of the late Reverend Forrester Caitland of Sioux Falls, South Dakota, who befriended my wife when she was alive and offered spiritual guidance in her time of need. And I

*request that Reverend Caitland erect a church on
my property in memory of my loving wife, Effie.*

Perspiration beaded on Dillon's forehead. Who
was Rachael Caitland? And why would Abel leave
part of his estate to a preacher? And why would he
ask to have a church built on his property in
Jasper when there was a perfectly good church in
Harley, only twenty miles away? Abel certainly
hadn't been a religious man.

*I bequeath my estate to these parties equally,
share and share alike, and hope they may live in
harmony.*

Dillon covered his face with his hands and
shook his head. What could Abel have been thinking?

The attorney plucked his wire-rim glasses from
his nose and rubbed the red imprint along the
bridge where they had rested. "You can contest
this," he said without preamble. "I understand
Abel was pretty sick the last year he was alive. He
was taking a lot of painkillers. Could have affected
his thinking."

Dillon pondered it as he stared out the window
of the attorney's office. It wasn't much of an office,
but then there wasn't much need for a fancy office
in Jasper, South Dakota, where the only attorney
in town worked one day a week and spent the rest
of his time in Harley. "Yeah, Abel wasn't himself,"
Dillon agreed.

"You want to fight it, then?"

Dillon shook his head. "No, I wouldn't feel right.
I consider myself lucky with what I have." Still,
what did he need with some goody-two-shoes who
probably didn't know the first thing about ranching? "Maybe she'll change her mind about staying
when she finds out she's sharing the place with

two men. I could always try to buy her out," he added.

"You can't afford to buy her out," the attorney told him. "The money, as I read from the will, has been split right down the middle. Which means you're going to have one heck of a time paying your bills this spring." He tapped his pencil on the desk as he spoke. "I doubt any minister would pass up the chance to build a new church, so she'll probably be on her way here as soon as she's informed."

But Dillon was only half listening. He was still reeling from the news and wondering how he would handle a woman living on the ranch, especially a minister. "I'll think of a way to get her to change her mind," he finally said, settling his gray Stetson on his head. He grinned suddenly, showing a mouth of straight white teeth. It was the same smile that had won him dances with the women at the Mustang—and more.

"Before I'm finished with her, she's going to think she's done met up with the devil himself."

One

The man appeared to be dead. Sprawled on a rickety rocker with his boots propped on the porch rail, and his head lolling to one side uncomfortably, he made not a move. He looked as though he'd been there for some time. Rachael took the steps leading to the front porch slowly. She couldn't imagine a man purposely falling asleep outside with the mid-March temperatures still dipping dangerously low.

His pewter-gray Stetson had been pulled down on his forehead, obscuring his eyes but offering a clear view of his nose and cheekbones and a square jaw that obviously hadn't met with a razor in days. His hair was as black as freshly mined coal and coarse as hemp, and fell past his collar—too long for her liking. She studied his face. Not a handsome one, she decided—too rugged and weatherworn. A man would have to have spent a lifetime on the prairie to have earned skin like his. Rachael thought of her own fair complexion that had never had much tolerance for sun while this man looked as though he'd literally baked in it. His hands were also tanned, she noticed. They were nice, though, she thought. His fingers were long and tapered and feathered with the same blue-black hair that covered his head. Powerful hands, she decided, noting the network of veins that ran just under his skin.

"You like what you see, lady?" a voice drawled lazily.

The sound startled Rachael so badly, she jumped. One hand flew to her chest as though she half expected her heart to leap right out into her palm. "Excuse me," she said. "I thought you were asleep . . . or something."

The man shoved the brim of his Stetson upward and gazed at her with midnight-black eyes. "Obviously."

Rachael blushed till the tops of her ears burned. Had she really been staring so blatantly, she wondered. Of course, it was his clothes that had captured her curiosity. He didn't dress like a man of the nineties or anyone else she knew for that matter. In fact, he looked as if he'd just stepped off the set of *Gunsmoke*, with his tight jeans and knee-length boots and faded bandanna.

There was humor in Dillon's voice when he spoke. "It's gettin' to where a man isn't safe on his own front porch," he said, his drawl thick as maple syrup.

Rachael snapped her head up as indignation and embarrassment filled her blue eyes. "I assure you that you're quite safe with me, sir." She wasn't sure which irritated her most, the way he made fun of her or his pronounced drawl. He obviously wasn't native to South Dakota. "If you'll just tell me where I can find Dillon McKenzie, I'll let you go back to your nap," she said tightly. She noted the pint-size whiskey bottle at his feet and her irritation grew. The man hadn't been napping; he'd been sleeping off a drunk! She knew the signs well since she counseled men who drank to excess.

Dillon unfolded himself from the rocker and stood before her, then doffed his hat. "You're looking at him, ma'am."

"You!" It sounded like an accusation.

"And who might you be?" But he already knew. He'd been expecting her.

"Rachael Caitland," she said. "*Reverend* Rachael Caitland," she added with much aplomb, "from Sioux Falls. I believe you knew I was coming?" She held her breath for his reaction. She'd had no idea what to expect or whether she would even be welcome.

"So you're the good reverend who has come here to save our souls, huh?" he said, taking a moment to study her. She was about as plain as they came, he decided. Her cornflower-blue eyes and thick brown shoulder-length hair were her only redeeming qualities. He could not help but feel a bit disappointed. If he was going to have to share his place with a preacher lady, he wished she could have at least been beautiful to look at.

"I expect I ought to warn you it won't be fun. I got breeder bulls who are easier to get along with than some of the ranchers out here."

"And are you as difficult to get along with, Mr. McKenzie?" she queried.

His lips twitched at the corners. "No, ma'am. As long as folks don't bother me," he added. "You rub my back, and I'll rub yours, so to speak."

Rachael was tempted to tell him there would be

no back rubbing while she was there. She shivered, and she didn't know if it was from the cold or the way he looked at her, his eyes knowing and amused, as though he shared some private joke she was not privy to. "Perhaps we could go inside," she suggested, huddling inside her heavy wool coat. "I'm not as accustomed to the cold as you obviously are."

Dillon leaned over and grasped the half-filled bottle at his feet. "This'll warm you up, ma'am, if you don't mind the taste."

Perfect red spots brightened both of Rachael's cheekbones. She sniffed and drew herself up as tightly as a wound rubber band. "I wouldn't touch that with a ten-foot pole, Mr. McKenzie."

He shrugged. "Yes, well, I woulda never offered it to you, but I noticed the way you kept staring at it like you wanted a sip."

She was clearly rattled by the remark. "I was just . . . surprised to find someone drinking at such an early hour."

"It's a long way from town, ma'am. It gets lonely out here on the prairie, nobody to talk to, nobody to—" He stopped but his meaning was clear. "A man's got to do what he has to do to get by. You'd be surprised what you'll do to keep from going crazy out here."

"You have no wife, Mr. McKenzie?" she asked, already dreading his answer. Why hadn't she thought of that before?

"No, ma'am. Not many women would want to spend their lives out here in the middle of nowhere."

Rachael thought he was being overly dramatic. "You talk as though you live at the ends of the earth," she said matter-of-factly. "I just drove through a very nice little town. And I noticed there were other ranches on the way. Surely you don't *have* to be alone."

"You're right, ma'am," he said, nodding thoughtfully. "Maybe I just use it as an excuse to drink." As if to prove his point, he unscrewed the cap on the bottle, raised it to his lips, and took a swig. He smacked his lips loudly and wiped them on a jacket sleeve before recapping the bottle. The woman before him stared back in horror.

"Something wrong, ma'am?"

Rachael merely shook her head. She would only make matters worse by taking him to task over his drinking, so she kept her mouth shut. There was time for that later. "I'm just cold," she said instead.

"Then I'm going to get you inside so you can warm up," he said, and stuffed the small bottle inside his coat pocket. He crossed the porch and dragged the battered screen door open. It squeaked like an injured bird in protest. "After you, ma'am," he said, jostling the heavy oak interior door and finally shoving it open with one shoulder. "Doors need fixin'," he added simply.

Rachael offered him the closest thing she had to a smile as she stepped inside the house that had been built to resemble an oversize log cabin. Her smile faded as she caught sight of a cluttered living room and a man sleeping facedown on the sofa, still wearing his hat and boots and snoring loud enough to rattle the windows. One arm was flung out in sleep and now rested on a coffee table littered with potato chip bags, beer cans, and empty peanut hulls. Nearby, an ashtray had been overturned on the dull plank floor, spilling cigarette butts everywhere. Obviously no one had seen fit to pick it up.

"That's Coot," Dillon said, nodding toward the sleeping man as he kicked the door closed behind him. It slammed loud enough to make Rachael jump but did not wake the man on the sofa. Dillon shucked off his jacket and tossed it carelessly onto a faded floral print recliner. The jacket slid from the chair and fell to the floor with a dull thump, but Dillon didn't seem to notice. "We sort of had a rough night last night."

"Oh?" Rachael was certain it had something to do with the whiskey bottle on the front porch and the beer cans on the coffee table. "And do you often have *rough* nights, Mr. McKenzie?" Her voice sounded judgmental, she knew.

It took every ounce of willpower Dillon could muster to keep from grinning. He wasn't about to tell her he and Coot had spent much of the night chasing down one of the breeder bulls that had broken through the fence. Let her think the worst. In fact, he was counting on it.

"Some nights it's harder to fall asleep than others, if you know what I mean," he whispered, leaning close enough so she could hear him and get a whiff of the whiskey he'd drunk for her benefit. "I wouldn't normally tell a woman such a thing, but with you being a preacher and all, I'm not ashamed to confess something so personal."

Rachael was accustomed to hearing confessions, but she did not want to hear his. With this man it was different somehow. "I see," she said. Her gaze drifted to his chest, noting the way it strained against the fabric of his shirt, as did his arms and biceps. His shirt lay open at the collar, and the V between was shadowed with black hair. There was power there, raw and masculine, and she wondered for the first time about her decision to come.

"Can I take your coat, ma'am?" he offered.

Rachael hesitated, feeling awkward at having to remove any item of clothing in front of him. She wanted to keep as many barriers in place as possible. But that was silly, she told herself, and shrugged out of the coat anyway. She handed it to him, and he draped it over the back of the floral chair.

"Are there *any* women on the ranch, Mr. McKenzie?" she asked, desperation creeping into her voice now. "A housekeeper maybe?" The question sounded absurd in her own ears. One only had to look at the place to see there was not.

"No." His gaze locked with hers in silent challenge as he said it. "Just me and Coot."

"I see," she repeated, for no other reason than she honestly didn't know what else to say.

The way she said it, with resignation in her voice, told Dillon that while she wasn't overjoyed with the news, it wasn't likely to send her scurrying away like a frightened jackrabbit. He studied her closely, taking in the pristine navy-and-white sailor dress she wore, and tried to think when he'd ever seen a more homely outfit. The dress was too big for her and sagged against her thin shoulders like a bed sheet on a coatrack.

"Is something wrong?" Rachael asked, uncomfortably noting his scrutiny.

"I was just thinking those clothes won't be any use for you out here."

Rachael glanced down at her outfit self-consciously. She had lost weight in the year since her father's death, and most of her clothes swam around her. "I'll need to dress nicely when I visit people and hold church services," she said, reaching back to tuck a strand of brown hair behind her ears. She wished the man wouldn't stare so. And he stood much too close, close enough so that she could not help but smell the offensive whiskey on his breath when he spoke.

"Where you plannin' to hold services without a church?" he asked.

"In this room."

"Here?"

"Until a church is available." When he started to object, she added, "Abel gave permission in his will."

So she had read the will, Dillon thought. She had probably studied the fine print, as he had, to see if there was some way of getting around it. "You want a cup of coffee?" he asked after a moment.

It was on the tip of her tongue to tell him she didn't drink coffee, that she preferred hot tea, but something told her he would find it as amusing and out of place as her outfit. And she wanted to escape the dimly lit room where they were forced to stand close and whisper to keep from waking the man on the couch. Dim lights and whispers created an intimacy between them that she couldn't bear another minute. She longed for a bright, cheerful kitchen where they could sit with the table between them and speak normally. "I would love a cup of coffee," she said.

"This way."

Rachael followed him into a room that appeared to be in worse shape than the one she'd left. The linoleum floor probably hadn't seen a mop since the man himself had seen a razor. The kitchen counters were so cluttered, she had no idea what color they were, just as she couldn't make out the original color of the limp curtains hanging from the grimy windows. A sense of dread fell over her as she perused the old grease-splattered stove. She had desperately counted on this being the right move for her, the answer to her prayers. Now she wasn't so sure.

"Coffee'll be ready in just a minute," Dillon said once he'd filled a percolator with cold water, spooned coffee grounds into the metal basket, and plugged it in. He wiped his hands on a dingy dish towel and tossed it aside carelessly. It fell into a black skillet lined with cold gray grease. Rachael suppressed a shudder and watched him cross the room to a yellow Formica kitchen table. He took a seat in one of the chairs and propped his boots on another. "Have a seat," he said, indicating the chair beside him.

Rachael forced herself to smile and took the chair on the opposite side of the table instead, but if he thought her reluctance to sit beside him odd, he didn't give any indication of it. "Thank you," she mumbled.

"I know the place needs cleaning up," Dillon told her as though reading her thoughts. "Me and Coot don't have much time for cleaning when we come in at the end of the day."

He watched her closely as he spoke, waiting for some sort of reaction. Her eyes were deeply troubled, he noticed, and he took comfort in that fact. She didn't like it one bit. Not that he blamed her, of course. She would have to be crazy or desperate to want to live in such a place, and he was counting on her being neither. As she gazed at the room rather forlornly, he affected a sober tone. "I reckon we're lucky you came along," he added. Her gaze collided with his as he said it, and it took every ounce of willpower he had to keep a straight face. He wondered if she had any idea how difficult it had been for him and Coot to mess up the house so badly. They hadn't washed a dish since they'd heard she was coming.

Rachael shifted uncomfortably in her chair, feeling somewhat overwhelmed at the monumental task that lay before her if she stayed. It was the first time she'd used the word *if* in her thoughts. She had just assumed everything would work out. For months she had prayed for a solution to her problems, knowing in her heart she had to leave Sioux Falls and make a new life for herself. When she'd learned of the inheritance, she'd been convinced the Lord had sent a miracle her way. Why else would an old man leave half of his estate to the daughter of a minister who hadn't set foot on his property for more than thirty years? The attorney had told her that her father had counseled Abel's wife out of a deep depression after she had suffered several miscarriages and discovered she would never be able to have children. But to Rachael, it was a modern-day miracle just the same. When the Lord closed a door, he opened a window, she had learned as a child.

She had thought of nothing else but building her own church ever since. She had not bothered to investigate the facts surrounding the ranch but had acted on blind faith, feeling in her heart it was wrong to question a miracle. She had assumed there would be others living on the ranch, a wife or housekeeper, as well as several employees. She had not counted on sharing a house with two crusty, whiskey-drinking cowboys.

Perhaps the Lord was testing her.

Rachael pondured her situation further. As part-owner of the ranch, it would be only fair for her to perform her share of the work, and since she knew absolutely nothing of ranching, she would naturally assume the household duties. "Who took care of the house in the past?" she asked after a moment.

"Abel cared for it. He was too far gone with arthritis to climb on a horse or drive nails into fence posts. Coot and I did all that."

She clearly saw the challenge in his eyes this time, the same look he'd given her when he'd told her there were no other women on the premises. Did he expect her to tuck her tail and run in the opposite direction now that she'd seen the place? she wondered. The thought made her sit a bit taller in her chair. If the Lord were indeed testing her, she had no choice but to follow through and make the best of it. People always emerged stronger after a tough challenge, she told herself. Besides, miracles did not come along every day. She would have to prove herself worthy of receiving one.

Rachael squared her shoulders. "Yes, well, I should be able to handle it," she said, sounding more confident than she felt. "Of course, I'll be busy with church work as well. That will be my top priority."

Dillon leaned forward and spread his hands flat against the tabletop, his agitation growing over the fact that his plan didn't seem to be working. He would have to press harder, make a few demands. "All I ask is that you keep the coffee fresh and put hot meals on the table for me and Coot," he said. "We put in long hours every day, starting at five."

She swallowed. "That's A.M.?" The Lord obviously had a sense of humor.

He nodded. "And we have big appetites."

Rachael studied his hands as he spoke and noted once more how nice they were, his nails clean and neatly trimmed. It struck her as odd that the man could live in such squalor and still be particular about his fingernails. Something wasn't right. But she chose to ignore it for the moment, concentrating instead on the subject at hand and wondering if she should tell him she couldn't cook. If only the Lord had seen fit to drop a miracle in that direction, she mused silently.

"We like our dinner on the table at twelve sharp, and our supper at six. Think you'll have a problem with that?" She'd never go for it, he thought smugly.

"And breakfast at five A.M.," she reiterated, wondering how anyone could climb out of bed at that hour, much less put food in their stomachs. Yes, it was definitely a test.

"That's right. There's plenty of food in the cupboard right now, but we can stock up tomorrow in town. You and I have to sign some papers at the attorney's office and go by the bank. I'll knock off a couple of hours early so we can take care of it."

"Maybe you would like to make a list of the foods you and Coot prefer," she suggested.

"We're both meat and potatoes men. That's simple enough."

It would have been simple had she known how to *prepare* meat and potatoes, she wanted to tell him. She thought of her father. He had loved to cook when he was alive, had more or less made a hobby of it, surprising her with rich tarts and blintzes and strawberry crepes prepared with homemade whipping cream. As a result, she'd never had to do so much as boil an egg. Since his death her meals had consisted of canned soup, fruits, and cheeses, hardly the sort of thing she could expect to feed two hungry cowboys. But Dillon Mckenzie was waiting for an answer.

"I'll do my best, Mr. McKenzie," she said at last, offering him a brave smile. But in her heart she knew she was going to have to request a second miracle. It had taken a miracle to get her there, but it would take another to get her through it.

Two

Dillon didn't speak for a moment, instead he gazed at the confident-sounding woman and wondered what he'd ever done to Abel Pratt to deserve the fix the old man had left him in. If the same thing had happened to anyone else, Dillon would have had a good laugh over it—pairing off a couple of cowboys with a lady minister indeed! Who could have imagined such a thing? But it wasn't happening to someone else, it was happening to him, and he didn't think it a damn bit funny! On top of everything else, his conscience was bothering him over giving this woman such a hard time. He tried to concentrate on what he knew was the best alternative for all of them.

He clenched his jaw together tightly and ground his back teeth until they hurt. Nothing he'd said had so much as swayed her decision to stay. "It's a hard life," he said after a moment, trying to hide his mounting frustration, "but if everyone pulls his or her weight, it makes it easier on the next

man. Or woman," he added as his eyes uncon-
sciously shifted to her breasts. He didn't realize he
was staring until she crossed her arms as though
trying to protect herself from his gaze. He blinked
and raised his gaze to her face. Her eyes were
guarded and cautious, and he couldn't help but
wonder about certain things, things he had no
right to wonder about, especially since she was a
minister.

"So, you've never been married?" he asked,
changing the subject.

Rachael's gaze didn't falter, but her hands fidgeted unnecessarily in her lap beneath the table.
"No." He nodded, but she could see there were
more questions in his eyes. She could not fault
him for being curious, she supposed. Most people
were. And he was a healthy, virile man who'd
probably sown his oats early in life and was still
doing so. He would naturally wonder about her
lifestyle, wonder how she managed without a man.
Thankfully, he was polite enough not to voice his
questions aloud.

Dillon felt his conscience prickle again at the
thoughts that filled his head. It didn't seem right
that he should be thinking such things about a
preacher lady, but he couldn't glance into those
blue eyes without wondering if a man had ever
bothered to look closely and notice the tiny gold
specks and the way her irises grew darker around
the edges. And he couldn't help but notice how
delicate her throat was without wondering if a
man had ever pressed his lips against the hollow
there or kissed the length of her collarbone. The
percolator belched loudly, and he jumped. His
chair skidded across the floor and almost toppled
over as he shoved it away. He focused his concen-

tration once more on how he was going to get rid of her.

"How do you like your coffee?" he asked, pausing at the table.

Rachael glanced up at him, feeling small at the way he towered over her. She guessed him to be well over six feet. His shoulders, she noticed earlier, spanned the doorways. "Just black," she answered.

Dillon turned on his heels and walked over to the sink, thankful for something to do. He'd never cared much for churches or ministers. In his opinion they were all pious do-gooders who sat on pedestals and did a lot of finger pointing. He'd seen the way she had looked at him when he had taken a drink of whiskey on the front porch, her mouth pursed and drawn up as if she'd just sucked a fat garlic pickle. While he might not drink on a regular basis as he would like her to believe, he certainly wasn't opposed to tossing down a couple of beers come Saturday night. And if the good reverend thought he was going to change his ways just because she was there, she had better think again.

Rachael's eyes followed Dillon as he crossed the room. She couldn't help but notice the fine figure he made. He was what most women would call strapping, she supposed. His jeans clung to his hips and thighs like plastic wrap, emphasizing each smooth, taut muscle—and there were plenty of them. She felt her face warm at the thought. She forced her gaze away. It was one thing to look at a man appreciatively, but it was another thing to blatantly stare at a man's body and wonder what he looked like unclothed.

Rachael thought it odd that in twenty-eight

years she had never had to take herself to task for such thoughts. She might notice a man's eyes or face or hands, but she would never question those things she couldn't see, having been raised from birth to believe *those things* were reserved for the marriage bed. It shocked her to think she might enjoy seeing Dillon McKenzie in the shower— shocked her and made her blush so badly, she was sure Dillon noticed.

Dillon *did* notice the rosy blush on her cheeks as he placed a mug of hot coffee in front of her, but he had no idea what had set her off. He also noticed how badly her hands trembled as she picked up her cup, and his gaze narrowed curiously. "Are you okay?" he asked.

"F-fine," she managed, and the blush worsened, spreading over her entire body so that even her limbs felt hot and weighted. She wanted to run and hide. It was embarrassing, humiliating, to be reduced to such a state at her age, and, Lord help her, there wasn't a darn thing she could do about it. He wasn't making it any easier, though. The more he stared, the worse she blushed.

Dillon remained standing. He sipped his coffee and studied the woman from beneath a heavy-lidded gaze. "You want to see the rest of the house?" he offered somewhat reluctantly.

"Yes!" Rachael's chair raked across the linoleum floor as she all but bolted from it, desperately wanting to escape his bold stare and her own loss of control.

Dillon arched one thick brow in response. Something was obviously bothering her, but he didn't press. "I'll show you the upstairs," he said.

Rachael followed him out of the room and through the living room, where the man called

Coot still slept soundly. As she climbed the stairs behind Dillon, she tried to concentrate on her surroundings and not the man in front of her, who moved with an easy grace despite his size. At the same time, she hoped and prayed the rest of the house was not as bad as what she'd seen so far.

But the Lord had obviously decided to test her further, because the upstairs was worse than the first floor. Three bedrooms made up the top floor, she discovered, the largest containing a man's belongings and smelling of tobacco and the cologne Dillon wore. It, like the rest of the house, was in total disarray. Clothes hung from doorknobs, chairs, and bedposts, and several ashtrays were filled to overflowing. Rachael did not go in, but merely peered inside the door quickly. A bathroom across the hall boasted an old claw-foot tub that looked as though it had not been cleaned in her lifetime. She stepped inside.

Dillon paused at the bathroom door as Rachael studied the room with a critical eye. "It needs to be cleaned as well, but I think you'll find it serviceable." The room was dim, and he flipped the light switch on. Rachael jumped, and he wondered again at her nervousness.

She pushed aside the curtain at the window and looked out at the flat land surrounding the house. "How long have you lived here, Mr. McKenzie?" she asked.

Dillon leaned against the doorframe and studied her as the late-morning sun streamed through the window and touched her face. Her skin was flawless. "Seven years."

"You must like it."

"It's okay," he said, trying to keep his voice free of emotion. He didn't want her to know how much he liked it, that it had been the only home he'd ever known. He realized he should be telling her how hard ranch life was, how many chores had to be performed in a single day. He should be telling her how the wind whistled across the open prairie in winter and chilled a man's bones, and how he and Coot had to fight like dogs to keep the old place warm. He wanted to tell her how the nearest theater was on the other side of Harley, twenty-five miles away and that they sometimes ran the same movie for two months before changing it, and that she'd have to drive just as far to find a nice restaurant or have her hair done. He should be telling her these things instead of studying her profile, he told himself, instead of picking out the details of her body. But he found himself drawn to each line, trying to see what that shroud of a dress tried to hide.

"Is that the barn?" Rachael asked, breaking into his thoughts as she gazed out at a large weathered structure.

Dillon turned his eyes away for the second time and crossed the small room. He came to a halt beside her at the window and gazed across the winter pasture where the largest barn stood. In a few weeks it would be time for spring roundup, and he and Coot would move the cattle to another pasture in anticipation of mating season. "Yeah," he said, and he looked at her once more.

Rachael was uncomfortably aware of his closeness. The smell of his cologne wafted past her, but she could not move away without being obvious. "It's a big ranch," she said.

"Big enough." But not big enough for the both of them, he wanted to add. "How long have you been preaching, Rachael?" he asked instead, his curiosity suddenly getting the better of him. He could not imagine the fragile woman standing before a pulpit shouting prophecies of hellfire and damnation to a congregation. He thought of the few times he'd attended church in Texas with his mother, and he almost shuddered at the memory of the white-haired, hawk-nosed minister who'd scared his brothers and sisters half to death with his terrifying sermons. Rachael didn't look the type. She appeared gentle and quiet and poised.

Rachael was clearly surprised by the question, but surprised even more that he'd used her given name. It sounded different on his lips, and she found her gaze drawn to them. They were full and sensual, she thought. "Three years," she said, and felt the old familiar blush creep up her neck once again. She wondered if there would ever come a time when she could look at him without blushing or growing flustered. She hoped for their sakes she could. "I was the associate pastor for my father's congregation for two years before he died. I took over at his death."

Her skin was not only flawless, it was almost transparent, he noticed, catching sight of the tiny blue veins in her eyelids when she blinked. He thought of the ranchers' wives he'd met over the years whose skin was just as leathery as their husbands', and he couldn't help but appreciate Rachael's smooth, unblemished complexion.

"What made you decide to take up that line of work?"

It was a question she heard frequently. "I wanted to help people," she said. "I thought of going into nursing or becoming a social worker, but . . ." She paused. For some reason it was important he understand, especially since they would be sharing the ranch. Her usual pat answer seemed inappropriate. "Do you have any idea how many people are hospitalized every year and there's absolutely nothing wrong with them physically?" She wondered if he even cared. "I thought maybe if I helped people emotionally and spiritually, the rest would sort of fall into place."

"Folks here are going to have a hard time with the new minister being a lady," he said.

Rachael fingered the ecru lace edging of the faded curtain and wished she could move from her spot without appearing rude. "I know." She wondered for a moment if he knew the circumstances surrounding her decision to leave her old church. She couldn't imagine how he would have found out. "But I'll manage," she added on a lighter note. She offered him a brave smile, but inside she felt her stomach tighten at the prospect of being turned away again. Being a woman had been a definite problem for her when she'd taken over her father's church. As long as her father had been alive and in the foreground, the congregation had accepted her gladly. It was only when she'd actually taken charge that she'd had problems. And then there was the worry of trying to fill her father's shoes. Not an easy job, she'd discovered. She had been a poor substitute in their eyes. But she was not about to confess her story to Dillon McKenzie. Nor would she admit how frightened she was that it might happen again. "I have faith that everything will work out," she said after a moment.

"I hope it's enough."

Rachael didn't respond. She would have to deal with that problem when it came up. And she had no doubt it would. At the moment, though, there was a more pressing problem, one that had arisen as soon as she'd set foot in the house and discovered there were no other women on the premises, one that had become even more troublesome to her when she'd seen the bedrooms. She raised her eyes to his. She had put it off long enough.

"Mr. McKenzie, perhaps you and I should discuss the sleeping arrangements now."

Dillon had seen it coming long before she'd formed the question on her lips, long before she had peeked into the bedroom and guessed it was his. He'd known from the moment the attorney had told him the good reverend was coming alone that she would find fault with the sleeping arrangements. That didn't mean he was going to make it easy for her.

"What do you want to discuss about them?" he asked, being deliberately obtuse.

Rachael clasped her hands together in front of her and decided now was her chance to put some well-needed distance between them. She left him standing at the window and walked to the bathroom door. It seemed an odd place to be carrying on such a conversation, but she preferred it to the bedrooms, and she didn't want to go downstairs and have Coot overhear something she felt was personal and between Dillon and herself. "Well, we can't very well sleep under the same roof, you know. It wouldn't be—" She paused. "Proper."

That was a word he hadn't heard in a long time. To a man who'd had no qualms about going home with a woman he'd just met, it sounded foreign. Not to mention outdated. "You worry too much, Reverend. I don't make a habit of going into a lady's room uninvited."

The way he said it told Rachael he probably had enough standing bedroom invitations to see him into old age. "It's not you I'm worried about," she said. "It's other people. What they might think or say."

Dillon folded his arms over his chest and regarded her. "Oh, so you're into appearances."

"I have to be. It comes with the job." She said it as though she had always known it, had taken it for granted and never questioned it.

"And you don't mind?" When his question drew a blank look from her, he went on. "I mean, don't you resent it sometimes? Haven't you ever been tempted to do something a little crazy . . . take a few chances? Have you always done exactly what you were supposed to do?"

"Most of the time," she answered, knowing he would probably find the thought quite boring. No doubt Dillon McKenzie was a man who thrived on taking chances and wouldn't lose sleep over what people thought of him. She had never had that luxury. Having had a minister for a father, she had towed the line from birth. "There have been times I wanted to ignore the rules, though," she confessed after a moment, offering him a shy, almost wistful smile. "I never understood why I wasn't allowed to wear shorts in the summer like all my friends. It seemed silly that I had to wear dresses or slacks—and slacks weren't popular with my father either, but he eventually gave in." Her smile turned suddenly mischievous. "Of course I would slip around and wear shorts anyway, now and then, when I spent the night with a friend."

Dillon grinned at the small confession and for a moment forgot he wanted her out of his house. "You really were a brazen little thing, weren't you?"

He wondered if that was the worst sin she'd ever committed and thought it rather refreshing.

Rachael laughed, and for a moment she forgot they stood on opposite sides of the fence. "And, of course, I wanted to attend school dances in high school when I got older, but that was out of the question too."

"You've never danced with a man?" he asked in disbelief. "What could possibly be wrong with that?"

Her smile faded slightly, and her gaze wavered. "You've danced with women, Mr. McKenzie. Are you going to tell me you've never felt anything?"

He appeared confused. Finally, he understood. "Oh, you mean sexual urges." She blushed profusely this time, and he was clearly amused by both the topic of their conversation and her obvious embarrassment. He could not imagine anyone living by such old-fashioned standards. And he couldn't remember the last time he'd seen a woman blush. "This is probably going to shock you, Reverend, but I don't have to dance with a woman to want her. I can get turned on simply by looking at her. And I don't have to grind my pelvis against her to know she's going to be soft and curvy in my arms. I have a fairly vivid imagination, you see."

She didn't doubt it for an instant, but it was not something she wished to pursue. She offered him a dainty sniff that told him she found his comments somewhat offensive. "Well, we are getting off the subject entirely," she said, and the girlish smile disappeared from her face without a trace. She was, once again, *Reverend* Caitland from Sioux Falls. "I merely brought all this up to make you understand that while some of the restrictions

I place on myself may seem silly and insignificant, I adhere to them just the same. I can't very well set an example for others if my own behavior isn't above reproach."

He pondered it. "But if you don't always agree with it and do it anyway, that would make you sort of a hypocrite, wouldn't it?" He was having fun with her now, although it would have been impossible to prove by his sincere manner.

"Certainly not!" she said, indignant that he would even suggest such a thing. "These restrictions are trivial when one looks at the big picture."

"The big picture?"

"Eternity, Mr. McKenzie. Eternity."

"Yes, well, has a man ever *asked* you to dance, Reverend?" There now, he thought, that should frost her toes.

Her back went ramrod stiff. He probably thought she was too plain to interest a man, and she was surprised how much it hurt. But she would conceal that hurt, as she had concealed it from her congregation when it had been obvious they no longer wanted her. Dillon McKenzie would never know how close to the truth he'd come. True, she had never been invited to dance. That didn't mean she hadn't dreamed of it. "There is no excuse for rudeness, Mr. McKenzie," she said, and headed for the door.

"And there's no excuse for you trying to cram your beliefs down another person's throat," he told her.

She paused in the doorway and turned. "I wasn't trying to."

Dillon closed the distance between them, coming to a halt only a few inches from her. He'd had enough of this teatime chitchat, and he was wasting a perfectly good Sunday. "But you *are* asking me to move out of my own house simply because you're worried what people will think, when you know damn good and well I couldn't care less. That's what this is really about, isn't it?"

Her gaze didn't waver from his. "Yes."

"Then why don't you come right out and say it instead of giving me this hogwash about school dances and summer wear."

"I was merely trying to make you understand why I feel the way I do about certain things, that's all. We're going to be sharing this ranch, maybe we *should* try to come to some sort of understanding."

"That isn't going to happen, and you know it. We're too different. I care only about this ranch and making it work. Do you have any idea how tight it's going to be trying to maintain this place now that the funds have been divided up to build a church?" He was getting angry now, but he couldn't help it. He became angry every time he thought about it.

She sniffed. "Surely you're not implying your cows are more important than the souls of this community."

"See, you and I don't even come close to understanding each other," he said, shaking his head.

"Yes, but I'm willing to try if you'll give me half a chance." She paused. "Tell me something, are you always this . . . testy?"

He caught the scent of something nice. It made him think of the smell of spring flowers carried across the prairie on a cool breeze. It made him even madder because he didn't want to like the way she smelled or enjoy hearing her laugh. He didn't want to notice how smooth her skin was or how the sun, streaming through the bathroom window, brought out the reddish-gold highlights in her hair. Besides, she had no business smelling so good, she was a minister. And he had no right enjoying it, because it was his job to get rid of her. That thought made him more determined than ever to see it through.

"I only act this way when I have a hangover," he said, "and I've got one helluva hangover this morning. You aren't making it any better with all these rules you're laying on me."

"Is this something you suffer from frequently?"

The look he offered her was smug. "As often as I can, Reverend. Does that shock you?"

"Not in the least."

Which meant he would simply have to try harder, he told himself. "I also smoke, gamble, cuss—" He tilted his head forward until they stood nose-to-nose. "And every now and then I drive up to the video store and rent a dirty movie. Triple X rated," he added for emphasis.

She responded with an indifferent shrug. He was obviously trying to get to her. She would not give him the satisfaction of thinking he had succeeded. "Why should I concern myself one way or the other with your lifestyle?" she asked in a bored tone.

He didn't hesitate. "Because you need to realize exactly what you're getting yourself into, that's why. Who knows what might happen to an innocent young thing like yourself way out here?"

"I'm not so young. Nor innocent."

"What if I lose control after a night of dirty movies and whiskey? What if I forget myself?"

"That's enough." She turned for the door, but he

stopped her in her tracks, positioning himself between her and the hall outside.

"Who'll protect you, Rachael? Certainly not Coot, who is half-deaf and wouldn't hear you call out for help."

Rachael felt the tension coil low in her stomach. Was he really threatening her? she wondered, looking intently into his dark eyes. It was hard to believe they'd laughed together only a few minutes before, that she'd almost felt comfortable with him. "I can't imagine why you're saying these things to me," she said, "but I assure you I'm not afraid. If you hope you'll convince me to change my mind about staying, you're wrong. I have a mission to perform here, and I plan on following through until the end."

The attorney was right, Dillon thought grimly, she wasn't going to give in.

"And another thing," she said. "You don't shock me one bit with these confessions of yours. I've heard it all. In fact, your stories are rather dull compared to most."

Dillon flinched. Dull? Did she say dull? He'd been called a lot of things in his life but never that. He studied her. She was obviously no shrinking violet as he'd first suspected. As a pastor, she *had* probably seen and heard every shocking sin ever committed. His own sins would seem insignificant compared to those she would have discovered in a large city. The smile on her face was confident and knowing. She was laughing at him. Laughing!

"So you find me dull, huh?" he finally said, stepping even closer. He backed her against the door and refused to budge, even when his thighs brushed hers, even as his wide chest pressed against her soft breasts. He had the supreme satisfaction of seeing that smile fade from her face as he anchored his wide hands against the door on either side of her head. "I'll show you dull, lady," he muttered.

Rachael didn't move from her spot because to do so would prove to him that he *did* frighten her. She gazed at him squarely, her blue eyes defiant, as his face moved nearer to her own. She stiffened suddenly. Surely he wasn't going to do something insane like kiss her, she thought. Panic gripped her, but before she could do anything about it, his lips captured hers with such force, her head was pressed back against the door.

His mouth was warm and whiskey flavored, but not at all unpleasant as she would have expected. Her lips parted in surprise, and Dillon used it to his advantage, prodding them even wider with his tongue. He played a delightful game of cat and mouse with her tongue as he deepened the kiss and bracketed her head between his palms so she couldn't move. Rachael was stunned motionless.

Then, it was over as quickly as it had begun, and he stepped away from her with that smug grin on his lips. All she could do was stare at him, wondering how on earth the kiss had happened and why she hadn't stopped it, and why she wasn't reprimanding him right now.

Dillon took great pleasure in the rosy blush on her face and the shocked look in her eyes. Her bottom lip trembled, and when she covered her mouth with her hands, he noted how badly they shook. "Don't ever call me dull again, Rachael," he said. "Next time I may ask for more than a kiss."

He left her then, left her leaning against the

doorframe weak and shaking and more confused than she had ever been in her life. What had she gotten herself into? she wondered frantically.

Dillon moved into the bunkhouse that afternoon.

Three

The sky was still pitch-black when Dillon nudged Coot awake the following morning. "Get up, Cooter, ol' boy," he said. "Breakfast in half an hour."

The sleeping man on the vintage iron bed, was barely visible tucked beneath a mountain of quilts sewn years before by Abel's wife. Although the quilts were now faded and frayed around the edges, they still kept a man warm in a house where the heating system had never worked properly. Dillon hoped to replace it one day, just as he hoped to replace the one in the main house—and put down new linoleum in the bathrooms and kitchens and patch the roof and do a dozen other things. But those repairs would have to wait, he knew, as would the tractor he needed so desperately, since he would have to divvy up the money with Rachael for her church, a church that probably wouldn't draw more than a handful of members.

The thought made him go tense all over, and he reached for the lamp switch on Coot's nightstand and switched it on. "Get up, Coot," he said, this time a bit more gruffly.

Coot grunted and mumbled something incoherent in his sleep, then pulled the covers to his chin as though seeking warmth. Dillon shook him. The older man opened his eyes one at a time and gazed at Dillon sleepily. "What time is it?"

"Four-thirty."

"Aw, damn, Dillon. What d'you mean waking me up at this godforsaken hour? Are you crazy?"

Dillon tried to quell his impatience. "I explained it all to you last night," he said. "If you hadn't sat up half the night watching David Letterman, you wouldn't be so tired." He was tired as well, but it wasn't from watching television. He'd lain awake half the night thinking about the woman who now occupied the very room he himself had been sleeping in before she'd arrived—and thinking about that kiss.

He would have been a liar to deny the fact that the kiss had weighed heavily on his mind. He shouldn't have done it, he told himself. Not only because she was a pastor, but because it was difficult to view her as *the opponent* when all he could think about was how good she'd tasted, how good it had felt. Simply put, he'd enjoyed the hell out of it. And he had no business kissing a preacher lady and liking it!

Coot pushed himself into a sitting position on the bed and rubbed his eyes with the balls of his hands. His red hair, untouched by gray despite his advance into middle age, was as neatly combed into place as it had been when he'd climbed into bed the night before. But then any cowboy who'd ever shared a bunk with Coot Jenkins knew that he was asleep as soon as his head hit the pillow. He never tossed and turned in bed, never so much as rumpled the bed covers, and come morning there was seldom a hair out of place. But also come morning, it was next to impossible to wake him as Dillon had discovered when Coot had signed on three years before. Coot slept like the dead, and it was the dickens trying to rouse him. But Dillon overlooked it because Coot was honest and hard-working.

"You're worse'n my third wife, Dillon, you know that? She used to get up with the chickens too."

"Yeah, well, this is important, Coot. Now, where are your pants?" Dillon reached for a pair of jeans draped over the foot of the bed. "Here, put these on." He dropped them onto Coot's lap.

"Now you're beginning to sound like my mother," Coot said. He kicked off the bed covers and stood, dressed in thermal long johns that clung to his birdlike legs. He shivered fitfully. "I don't see why we're botherin' to go over there, when you're so sure she won't even be up," he grumbled, stepping into his jeans.

"Because I want to see the look on her face when we drag her fanny out of bed this morning, that's why. And then I'm going to remind her how she agreed to pull her weight and—"

"You seen my socks?" Coot interrupted. "The ones I wore yesterday?"

"Yesterday? You're going to wear the same socks you wore yesterday? They're going to stink to high heaven, Coot."

"All my clothes smell. You won't let me wash them, remember?"

"That's because I want *her* to do the wash from now on."

Coot located his socks under the bed and slipped them on his feet, then stuffed his feet into a pair of worn leather boots. "I don't know why you're so hell-bent on getting rid of the lady," he said. "She seemed nice enough to me yesterday. Spoke to me a bit when I got up off the couch. Although I will admit she talks rather loud and stands right in my face as she does it."

"That's because she thinks you're hard of hearing," Dillon said. At Coot's questioning look he went on. "It's a long story. Just do me a favor and let her think it for a while."

Coot shook his head as though having great difficulty figuring his friend out. "I don't know why you don't just accept her. Maybe it'll do us good to have a woman in the house."

"When I'm ready to bring a woman into my house, *I'll* choose who it's going to be. But right now I don't have time for one, especially a woman who doesn't know the first thing about ranching. She's going to be in the way."

Coot reached for a flannel shirt hanging on a hook near his bed. "It's part hers now, Dillon. I don't see where you got much say in the matter."

But Dillon looked determined. "Give me time. I'll think of something." Then his look changed to impatience. "Aren't you ready yet? You take longer to dress than most women I know." Sometimes it was hard to believe they were best friends, Dillon thought. Especially after a long winter when the cold forced them to spend time together in close quarters.

"Mind if I brush my teeth?" Coot asked, obviously growing irritated.

"Don't go to a lot of trouble. As soon as we drag her out of bed, we'll come back here and sleep for a while. I'll let you sleep until seven, how's that?"

Coot paused at the bathroom door. "How long you plannin' to keep this up?"

"As long as it takes, Cooter," he said, his tone more sure than ever. "As long as it takes."

Five minutes later they left the bunkhouse and picked their way across the yard toward the main house. It was dark and cold, and the wind howled across the prairie in an eerie way.

"There are lights on in the house," Coot pointed out as they drew nearer.

Dillon shrugged off the remark. "That doesn't mean anything. She probably got scared during the night with the wind and all." He grinned. "And worrying about coyotes." He still remembered how Rachael's eyes had widened when he'd warned her to watch out for them before he'd carried the last of his belongings to the bunkhouse.

Coot glanced at him. "There ain't no coyotes around here."

"Yeah, well, she doesn't have to know that."

The men climbed the steps to the front porch a minute later. "Now, let me handle this," Dillon said. "I may have to talk a bit rough to her, shake her up, so to speak, but it's for her own good. There's no sense prolonging this. The sooner she realizes what a mistake she made coming, the better." He reached for the doorknob and frowned when he found it unlocked. "You'd think she would have at least remembered to lock the doors before going to bed last night," he muttered.

Dillon shoved the door open, and both men stepped into the house, pausing inside as the smell of fresh coffee, fried ham, and pine cleaner greeted them. They glanced at each other questioningly as they shucked their coats, draped them over a chair, and crossed the room to the kitchen.

They found Rachael standing at the kitchen sink, immersed to the elbows in fluffy white soapsuds and humming "How Great Thou Art" as she worked. As though sensing their presence, she glanced over one shoulder and smiled.

"Good morning, boys," she said cheerfully. "I didn't hear you come in. Would you like a cup of coffee?" She didn't wait for them to answer as she rinsed her hands and dried them on a paper towel, having already stuffed all the dingy dish towels into the washing machine to soak in bleach water. She would've had to be blind not to notice how surprised Dillon was to find her up and about.

It had not been easy climbing out of her warm bed at four, especially after having lain awake until well after midnight worrying about her situation, and the kiss she and Dillon had shared. But she had promised herself she would not dwell on that kiss, nor would she read more into it than was meant. Dillon had hoped to frighten or intimidate her, nothing more, and she would be foolish to think otherwise. Of course, there could never be anything between them; the mere thought was ludicrous. And she wouldn't be having this conversation with herself if she weren't so desperately lonely to begin with. She had never been so alone, had never craved simple human contact so fiercely. Her father's death and the ultimate rejection of her congregation had affected her deeply, she knew. But she had to get past all that now, had to move on with her life, as she had so often told those she had counseled when they'd suffered a loss.

Rachael gave none of her thoughts away as she poured Dillon a cup of coffee and handed it to him. She didn't quite meet his eyes as she did so, fixing her gaze instead on his chest, which strained against the teal-green flannel shirt he wore. His long legs were encased in denims, which were worn and faded to a cottony sheen, the hems slightly frayed where they brushed against his black leather boots.

Dillon took the cup, careful not to touch the delicate hand that offered it, for fear that he'd think about the kiss they'd shared the day before. He'd wasted enough time and energy on that thought. He pulled the cup away quickly, almost sloshing the coffee as he did so, and stepped back.

Rachael turned to Coot and spoke so loudly, both men jumped. "How do you like your coffee, Mr. Coot?"

Coot quickly regained his composure. "I'll take a little milk in it, if you got any," he answered.

Dillon watched from the corners of his eyes as Rachael prepared the other man's cup, still amazed that she was up and that she looked so put together at such an early hour. The full-length apron she wore was crisp and white, tied snugly at her waist. He was surprised to find her in jeans, but unlike his own, hers were neatly pressed, as was the cranberry blouse she wore, which brought out the flush in her cheeks. Her hips were fuller than they'd appeared the day before in a dress that was too large, and he couldn't help but gaze at them appreciatively as she worked. She was a bit on the slender side, he noticed, but he knew women who dieted themselves silly to achieve that look. Still, she managed to fill out the front of her blouse and the back of her jeans in a way that made him want to look a bit longer than good manners dictated.

As though sensing Dillon's eyes on her, Rachael glanced up. Their gazes locked, and for a moment they each waited for the other to speak. Dillon cleared his throat. "How'd you sleep?" he asked, feeling the need to say something, *anything*. He knew it was guilt prodding him to inquire about her. And he *did* feel guilty. Not for wanting to be rid of her but for stooping to the level he had, for using the threat of sex to scare her off. He had attacked her *personally* by doing so, had crossed a line that he should never have crossed. He still couldn't believe he had actually gone and kissed her, a *reverend* of all things!

Rachael smiled. "I slept fine, thank you. No problems with coyotes," she added, a teasing lilt to her voice. Coot chuckled, and Dillon shot him a dark look.

"If you boys will have a seat at the table, I'll serve breakfast," she said, still smiling as though she found something amusing. But her smile faded when she turned back to the stove. The scrambled eggs had not turned out right, and she'd burned the ham. She only hoped the men wouldn't notice.

Dillon and Coot shuffled to the kitchen table, each holding their coffee cup, while Rachael fumbled with the pans on the stove. Dillon raised his cup to his lips and sipped, then frowned. He looked into his cup curiously. "What happened to the coffee?" he asked. "It tastes like . . . cleanser."

Rachael, coming across the kitchen with a skillet of eggs, halted. "I scrubbed the coffeepot this morning," she said. "It was so badly stained, I couldn't see how to measure the water properly. Maybe I didn't rinse it well enough?"

"It tastes fine to me," Coot said, and was awarded another scowl from Dillon.

"I'll make a fresh pot while you eat," she offered, coming to stand next to Dillon. She smiled to hide her nervousness, but her hands trembled as she spooned eggs onto his plate. "I hope you boys like scrambled eggs," she said, trying to sound cheerful. "I certainly made enough."

Dillon gazed at the runny concoction on his plate and didn't quite manage to suppress the shudder it brought on. He glanced up at Rachael and found her watching him. "What's this?" he asked.

She tensed. "Scrambled eggs."

He picked up a fork and pushed them around on his plate and shuddered again. "Is this how they prepare eggs in the big city?" He tossed Coot a mischievous grin as he said it.

He was making fun of her. "Make your point, Mr. McKenzie," she said coolly.

"They don't look done."

"I don't like my eggs too done anyway," Coot offered from across the table.

"I was trying not to overcook them," Rachael said.

Dillon dropped the fork on his plate, leaned back in his chair, and shoved his Stetson high on his forehead. "You succeeded then. You didn't even come close to overcooking them."

Her face warmed under his mocking gaze. "I haven't had a lot of practice with eggs," she said. "I don't like them, so I don't often have to cook them."

"Ever thought you might like them if you *knew* how to cook them?" he inquired. She sniffed and hitched her chin high, and he knew he'd riled her.

"I'll take your eggs if you don't want them," Coot

said, reaching for Dillon's plate. Dillon didn't stop him.

Rachael turned to the stove and set the skillet on the burner loud enough to make Coot jump again. Dillon chuckled under his breath. So the good reverend had a temper, did she? Rachael returned a moment later and set a platter of fried ham onto the table. It was burned almost beyond recognition.

"You haven't had a lot of practice with ham either, have you?" Dillon said.

She sniffed.

"Exactly what *do* you know how to cook, Reverend?"

"I'm more interested in feeding a man's soul than his body," she replied matter-of-factly.

He nodded slowly as though giving it thoughtful consideration. "Yeah, well, that isn't going to do me and Coot any good out in the pasture today, is it? I mean, it *sounds* awful pretty, but a man can't perform hard work without nourishment."

"If you think you can do a better job, please don't let me stop you."

"Can't do that, Rachael," he said, his voice smooth as churned butter. "We made a deal, remember? If I were to back out and take over the cooking as before, I would be breaking my end of the bargain. And you being a pastor and all, you wouldn't have much respect for my word. Neither would Coot who works for me. So you see, as much as I'd like to help you out on this one, I can't risk having people think I don't hold up my end of a bargain."

"Mr. McKenzie, you're full of baloney."

Balancing his chair on its hind legs, he turned a

cocky gaze on her. "You really know how to cut a man to the bone, don't you, Reverend?"

"Would you like a slice of ham, Mr. Coot?" Rachael called out so loudly, it caused Coot to drop his fork with a clatter.

"Don't mind if I do, ma'am," he said, picking up his knife and stabbing a piece.

"I've also made toast." Rachael hurried across the kitchen and returned with a plate stacked high with toasted bread that she'd burned and had to scrape with a kitchen knife. She set it in the center of the table, then went back to the sink and concentrated on cleaning the percolator once more. And when she served them a second cup, Dillon wanted to tell her it still tasted like cleanser, but he didn't. He merely sat there, drumming his fingers against the table impatiently, while Coot consumed enough food and coffee for both of them.

"Don't you think you've had enough?" Dillon asked the man when Rachael poured yet another cup. "We *do* have ranch business, you know."

"I'll have another fresh pot ready when you come in at lunch," Rachael assured Coot, thinking maybe she could use vinegar to get the cleanser taste out of the pot.

Dillon shoved his chair from the table and stood, making Rachael realize, once again, how tall he was. His hat made him appear taller, somewhat formidable. "I'm going to knock off a couple of hours early today," he said, not quite meeting her gaze as he spoke. "You and I are expected at the attorney's office this afternoon to sign papers. We'll also need to go by the bank."

She nodded. "Good. I need to pick up groceries while we're there."

It was on the tip of his tongue to tell her what a waste of time it was to buy food when she obviously had no idea how to cook it. "We'll leave at three o'clock," he said instead, and strode out of the room. Coot followed, still chewing on the piece of toast in his hand.

Rachael heard them close the front door behind them a moment later. She sighed and sank onto the chair Dillon had occupied earlier, suddenly exhausted with all that had taken place since she'd climbed out of bed. She had not realized how tense she had been until that moment, and now she was almost weak with relief that they were gone, especially Dillon. She felt close to tears as she surveyed the dirty dishes before her and thought of all that needed to be done. How would she ever get the place in order by next Sunday so she could hold services? And when would she find time to go out and *meet* people so she could invite them? And what kind of church could she hope to build with the modest funds Abel Pratt had left her? She would have to be extremely frugal with her money, she realized, since she would have to oversee the expenses personally until her congregation grew. *If* it grew. But she wouldn't think of that right now. One thing at a time. Besides, the Lord had sent her for a reason. Surely He wouldn't have gone to the trouble if He'd planned to let her fail.

If only the Lord could teach her to cook, she thought, remembering how she had literally ruined breakfast, causing Dillon to start his day on an empty stomach, without even the benefit of a cup of coffee to warm him. She couldn't even toast bread without burning it to smithereens.

Guilt was a terrible thing to have to deal with after a sleepless night, she decided. And she *did* feel guilty, not only for ruining breakfast but for kicking Dillon out of his own house. She'd had no right, of course, it *was* half his. And it had been Dillon McKenzie who'd worked the ranch these past seven years, not her. She had come barging in as if she owned the place, looking down her nose at him for the way he lived, and had thrown him out like week-old bread. And there she was, cleaning the main house and getting it in shape for *her own* comfort, when what she really needed to do was clean the bunkhouse so they would have a clean place to come home to at the end of a hard day. It was only fair that she do that for them, since they were doing the ranch work.

Her mind made up, Rachael went into action, searching the lower kitchen cabinets for cleaning supplies and everything else she would need to get the bunkhouse in order. She poured vinegar into the percolator before she left so it could soak, remembering her promise to have a fresh pot of coffee waiting when the men came in for lunch.

Rachael stood before the bunkhouse a few minutes later, arms loaded down with her cleaning supplies, and she paused at the door before going in. She had no idea what she would find inside and only hoped it wasn't as bad as the main house. Near the door, a large black motorcycle with the name Trigger painted on it rested on its kickstand, and she had no doubt it belonged to Dillon. She opened the front door and stepped inside.

Rachael stood in the small but orderly living room and looked around. The furniture was a bit shabby, but serviceable. An old television set rested on a battered table near one wall, and a collection of magazines were stacked neatly on the coffee table. Balancing the box of cleaning supplies on one hip, she leafed through the magazines curiously and wasn't surprised to find several *Penthouse* magazines among the *National Geographic* and others on beef farming.

Rachael made her way across the room, feeling somewhat uncomfortable being there but determined to do the job she had set out to do. She found a tiny kitchen at the back of the house and was surprised it was as neat as the living room. The metal sink sparkled, as did the white counters and old linoleum floor that appeared to have been waxed recently. In one corner of the room, newspapers had been wrapped in twine and stacked meticulously. She set her box down and stared at the room. Something wasn't right, she thought, feeling like Dorothy in Oz. It was the same feeling she'd gotten when she had noticed Dillon's hands, his fingernails scrubbed clean and neatly trimmed, so out of character for a man who wore his hair too long and didn't shave. She spied the automatic coffee maker nearby, half-full and hot to her touch. The dirty cups beside it told her Dillon had not gone without coffee after all, as he'd let her believe. She felt the first stirrings of irritation and something else she couldn't quite put a name to.

Wearing a perplexed frown, Rachael walked from the room into a small hall and opened a door leading off of it. She simply stood there for a moment, one slender brow arched high on her forehead as she gazed at Coot lying on the bed, snoring fitfully, still wearing the clothes he'd had on at breakfast. Rachael stepped back into the hall and closed the door quietly. She paused only a moment before she pushed the door open at the opposite end. She was not at all surprised to find Dillon sprawled on the bed, one arm flung over his eyes. His bedroom, just as Coot's, was neat and uncluttered.

It didn't take her long to figure out exactly what was going on—the spotless bunkhouse, the way the men had returned to bed as soon as they'd made an appearance at breakfast to make certain she had gotten up—and when the realization hit her fully, anger surged through her body with the force of a freight train. She had been duped; played for a fool! And there was no doubt in her mind who had instigated the whole thing. No wonder Dillon was tired, she thought. It had probably taken him days to reduce the main house to a shambles before her arrival. And he'd probably had a ball doing it. She could imagine how he and Coot had laughed as they'd planned it. She clamped her lips together tightly as her irritation flared into a ball of heat in the pit of her stomach. Dillon McKenzie didn't want her there, that much was obvious. Just how far would he go to get rid of her? she wondered. She thought of the kiss and suspected nothing would stop him. He was as sneaky and underhanded and conniving as some of her church members had been, setting her up behind her back, hoping all the while she would fail. Well, she would show him she would not be so easily gotten rid of a second time!

Rachael stalked out of the room and into the kitchen and searched the cabinets until she found a large plastic pitcher. With grim determination, she filled it with cold tap water and marched back into the bedroom with the zeal of a marine sergeant.

She paused beside the bed and gazed down at Dillon's sleeping figure, her eyes almost glassy, the water pitcher thrust precariously over his wide chest. Because he rested with one arm still flung over his eyes, she could see only the bottom half of his face. He really was a handsome devil, she thought. If he were to clean himself up—shave and cut his hair—the look would be quite devastating. But this man was the enemy, she reminded herself, and he had pushed her too far. Even ministers had their limits.

"I wouldn't do that if I were you," Dillon said, shattering the silence in the room and startling Rachael so badly, she jumped and almost sloshed the water. His arm slid from his face and fell to his side casually, telling her he wasn't the least bit intimidated by her presence *or* the pitcher of water.

Rachael regained her composure almost immediately and hitched her chin high. "And why shouldn't I?" she demanded. "It's nothing less than you deserve after what you did to me, making me get up in the middle of the night to prepare your breakfast when you had every intention of going back to bed. Not to mention how you literally trashed the house for my benefit."

He looked unmoved by the fact she'd found him out. "I did it to teach you a lesson."

"Oh? And were you trying to teach me a lesson yesterday when you shoved me against the wall and kissed me?"

His gaze dropped to her lips at the reminder, and he studied them so intently, Rachael felt as though he'd kissed her again. She shivered involuntarily and was certain those black eyes hadn't missed it. "I simply thought you needed kissing," he said, drawing a great deal of satisfaction from her discomfort. "But that's nothing compared to what I'm going to do to you if you douse me with that water."

Rachael battled with indecision. Her behavior was clearly unbefitting that of a minister, and she would only be stooping to his level if she poured it on him. And what would people think if they learned she had walked into Dillon McKenzie's bunkhouse and done such a thing? It literally smelled of impropriety. She sniffed and lowered the pitcher, wishing she didn't have to worry about whether something was proper or improper and could give the man what he truly deserved.

"I knew you wouldn't do it," Dillon said, stacking his hands beneath his head and regarding her with a look of smug satisfaction. He crossed his long legs at the ankles and gazed up at her lazily, as though he had all the time in the world. "You're much too tame for something like that."

Which meant he found her dull and boring and predictable. Rachael went rigid at the sight of those amused eyes, the mocking curve of his lips. He was making fun of her again, as he had the day before when he'd ask her if a man had ever invited her to dance. He'd done nothing but make fun of her and trick her since she had arrived. "I think you underestimate me, Mr. McKenzie," she said.

She promptly raised the pitcher over his head and dumped it.

Four

Dillon came out of the bed with the speed and agility of an angry lion, sputtering and cussing and slinging water in every direction. Rachael dropped the empty pitcher and started for the door. Dillon stopped her, closing a fist around her wrist that felt like a steel claw. "Why you little—" His voice, low and ominous, sounded as though it had been conjured up from the depths of hell.

"Let go of me, Dillon McKenzie," Rachael ordered, fear making her sound more brave than she felt. What insane notion had made her think she could get away with such a thing? "You had it coming and you know it. Now we're even." She tried to pull away but it was useless.

"Hell no, we're not even," he said, backing her against the wall of his bedroom. "We're not even close."

"You tricked me!" she said. "You made me look foolish, not only to myself but to Mr. Coot." She tried to wriggle free, but he braced her against the wall with the lower half of his body. "You tried to frighten me."

"And you damn well *better* be frightened, lady," he all but shouted. He was standing so close, she could see the beads of water clinging to his eyelashes. "If you knew what I was thinking of doing to you at this very moment, you'd get down on your knees and pray for salvation."

"What would you know about salvation, Mr. McKenzie? You are the most unscrupulous man I've ever met!"

"You ain't seen nothing yet, Reverend. But then maybe that's what you came looking for in the first place. Why else would you be in my bedroom?" He pressed his body more tightly against hers.

Rachael gasped aloud at the intimate contact. "You've gone too far this time."

"I think that's exactly what you were hoping for when you came in here," he ground out between clenched teeth. "I think you liked that kiss so much yesterday that you decided to come back for more. Is that it, Rachael? Are you curious to find out if the rest is as good? I can certainly oblige you."

Rachael knew then that she had indeed made a grave mistake, and the thought frightened her. She had no idea what the man was capable of. Her face burned with shame at the way his body held hers fast against the wall, making her uncomfortably aware of his strength and maleness. His eyes bore into hers, stripping her completely bare of what thin layer of reserve was left. She felt small and vulnerable and no longer in control.

For the moment, she wasn't the steadfast Reverend Caitland from Sioux Falls intent on serving her Master. That cloak of protection had fallen away the moment Dillon McKenzie had closed his fist around her. At this moment, she was simply a woman, a woman whose body was being affected by this man's closeness. Tears burned her eyes as she fumbled for a reply to his accusation and those already churning in her mind, as she grappled with her body's eager awakening. Had she really been looking for this when she'd entered his room with that water pitcher? she wondered, and was shocked to think she might have been. And wasn't it sheer madness to enjoy this feeling of half fear, half anticipation that being close to him brought on?

"That's not why I came," she finally choked out, trying to prove as much to herself as to him. "I felt guilty for what I had done to you. For putting you out of your own house. I was simply trying to make up for it."

"By sneaking into my bedroom and pouring cold water in my face?" he demanded.

"I came in to clean the place for you. But when I saw how neat everything was and found you in bed, I realized you had tricked me." She swiped at her tears. "I know you don't want me here, but the truth is—" She hiccuped. "I have no place else to go."

Dillon didn't speak right away, he was too absorbed with the look on her face, which bordered on despair. He loosened his grip on her. "What are you talking about? You could always go back to Sioux Falls."

The tears pooled in her eyes and balanced on her bottom lid precariously before spilling onto her cheeks. "My congregation doesn't want me." She refused to meet his gaze as she said it, and it cost her everything to tell him. "I was forced to leave."

Fresh tears filled her eyes. "They didn't want a woman in the pulpit."

"Why didn't you stay and try to fight them? You don't look the type to give up."

"Because I was losing church members." She could barely speak for crying. "I thought it would be better to go instead"—more tears—"instead of forcing members out. People need a church."

Dillon was at a loss for words. He'd seen a woman cry before but never like this—desperate, heart-wrenching sobs that literally tore at his own gut and made him forget that he was angry with her and why. He had a sudden, insane urge to comfort her, take her in his arms and kiss away the tears. He resisted. Instead, he released her and stepped back, feeling an overwhelming need to separate himself physically and emotionally from her.

"Start talking, Rachael," he said in a deadpan voice.

"They wanted me out," she repeated, and raised the hem of her apron to her eyes. She dabbed them with trembling fingers. "As long as my father was alive and I took my place beside him, it was okay. But the older, more established members did not like it when I took charge." She sniffed. "They shot down all my ideas, my plans for a day-care center and singles program. *Everything.* I tried to ignore it, but after a while people were focusing more on the disharmony going on *inside* the church than what we were doing for the community."

"So you gave up?"

"You don't understand. It split the church. People started leaving. The choir director left and took several choir members. Some of my deacons even walked out on me. I could have stayed and fought,

I suppose, but what good would it have done if I lost half my congregation in the process?" She saw that he really didn't understand. "My job is to get people *into* the church, not run them off. So I resigned." She paused and wiped her eyes again. "Then, I got the call from the attorney here in Jasper telling me of the inheritance, and I thought everything was going to be okay."

Dillon wiped his face with one hand and remembered suddenly that he was wet, drenched actually, from the waist up. "Don't move from this spot," he ordered, and hurried from the room. He went into the bathroom, stripped off his shirt, and dried himself with a bath towel. He returned a moment later with the towel draped around his neck and went immediately to an old dresser where he fumbled through several drawers for a clean shirt.

Rachael watched him from across the room as he searched the drawers, her gaze lingering on his wide back, taking in each detail—the sinewy muscles in his arms, the flat shoulder blades, the slight, almost imperceptible indentations of his rib cage—and she could not look without appreciating. He plucked a faded blue work shirt from a bottom drawer and shook it, and those same muscles rippled from the effort. Rachael swallowed and looked away. She could not look at those smooth, taut muscles without wanting to touch them, test their firmness with her fingertips, feel the leathery texture of his skin.

It had to be wrong to want to touch a man so badly, she thought.

Dillon stuffed his arms into the shirt and faced Rachael once again, noting with some detached sense of amusement that she was doing everything in her power not to look at him. "We have to talk," he said.

Rachael's gaze drifted once again in Dillon's direction, and she caught sight of his wide chest, peeking out from beneath the slits of his shirt. She blinked. "I'd feel more comfortable in the kitchen."

Dillon cocked his head to the side as he closed the final button. "Whatever you say, Reverend."

Rachael led the way out of the room, going directly into the kitchen, where the sun spilled through the windows and gave the room a safe feeling. "Would you like me to pour you a cup of coffee?" she offered politely, feeling the need to occupy herself until he said whatever it was he thought needed saying.

"I'd just as soon you keep your hands off my coffeepot, Rachael." He chuckled at the dark look she shot him, and filled an earthenware mug. Then, he leaned against the cabinet and sipped for a moment in silence, but his black eyes never wavered from her face. "Abel must've been out of his mind to leave this place to the two of us," he mused aloud.

She nodded. "Yes, well, I've thought the same thing once or twice since I arrived," she confessed.

"So what are we going to do about it?"

Rachael met his steady gaze. Leaning against the cabinet with his shirttail hanging out and only his thick socks covering his feet, the scene was once again a bit too intimate for her tastes. His hair was damp and mussed from drying, and she wondered how he could look so good. "I think we need to make the best of it," she said. "It's like you said before, we both have an interest in the place. You want a ranch, and I want my church. There will have to be give-and-take."

"People are going to talk, Rachael." When his words drew a blank look from her, he went on. "It doesn't matter if you're a minister or not, you're still a single woman living on a ranch with two cowboys."

"Yes, but not under the same roof."

"And you think that matters?"

"Yes, I do." She couldn't help but wonder why he would bring it up to begin with, since he'd made it plain he didn't care what people thought of him. Unless, of course, it was another tactic to dissuade her from staying. "I can't control what people think, Mr. McKenzie. I can only control my own behavior and see that I act in a way that complements my vocation." She thought of the pitcher of water she'd dumped on his head and knew she had failed miserably in that particular instance. But Dillon McKenzie seemed to have a way of pulling at her more volatile side. "Which is why I asked you to move to the bunkhouse to begin with," she added, then paused. "Of course, there'll be those who will gossip regardless."

"So that leaves the problem of you and me and how we're supposed to get along."

The way he said it told her he wasn't going to bend over backward to see it happen. Rachael crossed her arms over her breasts and regarded him with a steadfast gaze. "Mr. McKenzie, I'm not going to continue defending my reasons for being here. I inherited this ranch equally. I promised to try and pull my weight, but I feel I should be able to live here peacefully and without harassment from you and your ranch hand."

"What are you trying to say in *real* language?" he asked, realizing with amusement that he'd managed to raise her ire again.

She sniffed. "I should not have to put up with offensive remarks about my cooking, nor should I have to live in a trash pile of a house simply because you want to make my job more difficult. I will try to see that the place is picked up, but as I told you before, my church comes first."

"And the cooking?"

"I'm willing to learn if you can be patient. But you have to give me a chance. Perhaps you could teach me."

His look turned to disbelief. "*Teach* you? When am I going to find time for that?"

"You'll have more time on your hands now that I'm taking over the housework and laundry. Besides, it was your decision that I take over those specific chores, you know. I could've just as easily come in and insisted on doing ranch work. Being cooped up in a dirty house isn't exactly my idea of a fun time."

"But you don't have the slightest idea how to do ranch work." He paused. "Do you?"

"I know as much about ranch work as I do cooking. The only difference is I would probably find that job more exciting than standing in a hot kitchen. Abel's will never specified who was supposed to do what, only that the care of the estate was to be divided."

Dillon knew for the first time in his life what real panic was. He had been foolish to think Rachael would come in and quietly assume the house duties simply because it suited him, when, in fact, she might find ranch work more to her liking. That's all he needed, he thought, some female trying to drive nails into his fence posts or stringing barbed wire or trying to lift bales of hay onto the back of his pickup truck and the million other things he did in a single day. If he thought she was in the way now, he could only imagine what she'd be like out in the pastures.

Dillon gritted his teeth at the smug look on Rachael's face. She knew what she was doing, the little witch. She knew he didn't want her out on the ranch with him any more than he wanted to be stuck doing housework at the end of the day. "That's blackmail, Reverend," he said.

Rachael hitched her chin high. "I prefer to call it negotiation."

Dillon couldn't help but chuckle at the challenging look on her face. Was this the same woman who'd sobbed uncontrollably a moment before? She was a hard one to figure out. For some strange reason it made him all the more determined to try. "Okay, Rachael, I'll teach you to cook," he said reluctantly, and was rewarded with a bright smile. "But I expect something in return."

"That doesn't surprise me." She hoped what he expected in return was legal and moral.

He seemed unperturbed by her remark. "Spring roundup is in a few weeks. That's when we bring the livestock in for branding and vaccinating. The other ranchers and I swap off the work so we don't have to hire a bunch of outsiders. I'll be expected to feed them when they come here. It's sort of a social event." He paused only briefly. "I'll teach you to cook, if you'll help me prepare food for the roundup and serve it for me."

Rachael nodded. She could handle it as long as she didn't have to do the actual cooking by herself. "That sounds fair enough. Let me know the date as soon as you have it, and I'll plan around it." She reached for her cleaning supplies. "Now, if that's all, I really must get back to work."

"One other thing," Dillon said, stepping closer. He laid a big hand on the box, preventing her from lifting it. "If we're going to try and live on this ranch together, I want to set a few ground rules."

"Such as?"

"You stay out of my way."

"I didn't realize I was *in* your way."

"What I mean to say is, you do your thing and I'll do mine. I don't want you interfering with my life. I don't answer to anybody, and that's the way I like it."

"We all have to answer to somebody sooner or later, Mr. McKenzie." She glanced heavenward, nodded curtly, picked up her box, and left.

Rachael was dressed and ready precisely at three, wearing a new black linen chemise that hugged her slender shape in a way that was feminine and eye-catching without appearing overly provocative. The simple pearl necklace and earrings that had once belonged to her mother were her most valued possessions and complemented the outfit nicely. While she waited for Dillon, Rachael surveyed the progress she had made that day on the house. She had taken down the curtains to wash them, cleaned and polished the windows until they sparkled, then scrubbed the floors and waxed them till they shone like a new car. Although there was a lot more to do, she felt she had tackled a few of the toughest jobs.

Dillon stepped into the house a few minutes later, scrubbed and cleanly shaven, dressed in new jeans, a clean navy shirt, and his heavy jacket. "Ready?" he asked. He came to an abrupt halt at the sight of Rachael, his eyes taking in her appearance in something akin to shock.

Rachael knew a moment of intense discomfort as Dillon perused her. "Is something wrong?" she asked, glancing down at her dress self-consciously. The way he was staring, she half expected to find she'd put it on wrong side out.

"You look different." It sounded like an accusation.

Rachael fidgeted with her necklace, trying to decide whether *different* was good or bad. "Yes, well, I wanted to try and make a good impression in town today." Still fingering her jewelry, she asked, "Do you think it's too much?"

Dillon wondered why he hadn't really noticed her legs before. They were long and slender and perfectly shaped. He followed her calves downward to her trim ankles and dainty high heels. Damned if Rachael Caitland didn't have knockout legs, he thought. His mind was filled with the sudden image of those same legs wrapped around his waist, and he blinked the small picture away quickly.

"No, you look fine," he said after a moment. Then, on an impatient note, added, "We need to get going." Without another word, he headed for the door. He couldn't very well spend the rest of the afternoon gawking at some preacher lady's legs, for Pete's sake!

They drove in silence. Rachael didn't try to break it. Instead, she concentrated on her surroundings. But she was uncomfortably aware of Dillon's presence and wondered if she would ever be able to share a room or the front of his truck with him without his body sending subtle messages her way. Would she always find it so difficult to meet that dark-eyed gaze of his, she wondered. Would she always find herself breathless when he was near? It wouldn't make for a comfortable relationship, she realized.

Before long they reached the town, which was nothing more than a handful of stores lining either side of the street, less than a city block in length. There was a grocery store, a feed and seed and hardware combined, a post office, and a video store on one side of the street, and across from it sat a large frame structure called the Mustang Bar and Grill, dwarfing the barbershop and coffee shop that flanked it. Not more than a hundred yards away was the fire department, a desolate-looking concrete building that housed a rather antiquated fire engine. The street had been widened to accommodate a median on which a wooden sign read: Welcome to Jasper.

Dillon turned off the main street and followed a narrow one until he came to a duplex that had been turned into a law office and a doctor's office. A battered ambulance shared the driveway with a pickup truck and Jeep. "This is it," he announced.

The business with the attorney took less than half an hour, after which Dillon drove to the Jasper City Bank, a mobile home with a drive-through window attached. "It's not much of a town," he said once they'd finished their transactions. "Most people do their shopping in Harley."

"There's no church in Jasper?" Rachael asked, unable to believe it.

"Used to be," he said. "It was struck by lightning last spring and burned to the ground before anybody could get to it. Most of the members started driving to Harley for services after that." He paused. "I understand Abel's wife used to invite ministers to come to town and hold services at the little schoolhouse on the ranch before they built the church."

Rachael smiled. "My father preached there when he was a young man," she offered, "long before I was born. I remember him telling me about it. Could you show it to me sometime?"

Dillon shrugged. "Sure, why not." But he was tired of talking about churches. What he really wanted to do was go into the Mustang, kick up his feet, and have a cold beer. He seldom took time to come into town during the week and wanted to take advantage of it.

"I would like to visit some of the shop owners and introduce myself," Rachael said after a moment. "Would you mind? It won't take long."

It fit right in with Dillon's plans. He pulled onto the main road and searched for a parking place. "I'll wait for you inside the Mustang and meet you back at the truck in an hour."

"You're not coming with me?" At the look he shot her, she hurried on. "I mean the people here know you and all. I was hoping you could introduce me." She knew it was unfair to ask but nervousness prodded her on.

Dillon didn't hesitate. "No, Reverend. I've already told you, you do your thing and I'll do mine. You're on your own." He parked, climbed out of the truck, and closed the door behind him. Giving her a brief impersonal nod, he strode away.

Rachael watched Dillon cross the street and felt her heart sink at the sight of his retreating back. He was right, she knew, she *was* on her own. She could not expect him to pave the way for her in this town, simply because she was afraid of being rejected again. She would have to prove herself to these people by doing the best job she could. Not only that, she had a lot to prove to herself.

Rachael climbed out of the truck, squared her shoulders, and headed for the barbershop.

From a window of the Mustang, Dillon watched Rachael exit the barbershop ten minutes later as he listened to Joe, the bartender, recount the fight that had brokenout the previous Saturday night after Dillon had gone home. Saturday night fights weren't uncommon at the Mustang as the night wore on. Which is why Dillon always left by midnight and spent an hour at the all-night coffee shop, where he could eat something and clear his head before making the long drive home. Unless, of course, he met someone he wanted to spend time alone with. But that was seldom the case these days, and he wondered if he was becoming too particular—or maybe cautious was the word.

Things sometimes got rowdy at the Mustang. Ranch owners and cowboys alike fought over money and women and anything else that came to mind once they'd had too much to drink. Some of them didn't know when to put the bottle down. After having lived with a father who drank too much, Dillon didn't enjoy being around it. But he enjoyed the easygoing camaraderie of the men, and women, and he supposed he liked feeling as though he belonged.

From his place near the window, Dillon watched Rachael walk into the video store, and he wondered with a grin what Clive and Eva Barker, the owners, would make of her. There was something different about Rachael today, but he couldn't put his finger on it. It had to be the dress, he decided as he studied her profile; the gentle sway of her hips, her pert breasts. She was not the sort of woman he would seek out on a Saturday night, but if a man took the time to look at her, he would not be disappointed. What he liked best about her, he supposed after a moment, was the fact that she was so uniquely feminine. In a day and age when women often felt they had to be strong and hard to fight for equal rights, Rachael was able to achieve the same goals without losing her womanly qualities. What could be more intimidating than trying to take a man's place behind the pulpit, he thought.

He was probably a cad for not going with her to break the ice with the townspeople, he thought, but he did not want to get involved in Rachael Caitland's problems. She had already talked him into teaching her to cook against his better judgment. Besides, he really didn't think she would last long in Jasper, and the less involved he got with her, the less guilty he'd feel when things didn't work out.

An hour later, Dillon exited the Mustang and crossed the street, heading in the direction of his truck. He saw Rachael standing in front of the grocery store talking to a group of ladies, and she waved excitedly when she spotted him. He went stiff all over.

He did not want Rachael carrying on in front of the whole town as if they were good friends. It was bad enough that folks would have to find out they were sharing the ranch—if they hadn't already found out from Coot, who couldn't be trusted to keep quiet about it. With Rachael herself running in and out of the stores and stopping people on the street to announce the fact, it was only a matter of time before everybody in Harley knew as well. The boys from the Mustang would get a kick out of it, he was sure. Of course they'd wonder among themselves if Dillon McKenzie wasn't somehow more involved with the preacher from Sioux Falls, and before long he wouldn't be able to show his face inside the bar and grill.

"I thought maybe we could buy groceries now," Rachael said, hurrying to meet Dillon once she'd excused herself from the group of women she'd been talking to. "If you have time," she added quickly, when she saw the scowl on his face.

His scowl deepened. "You mean now? Together?"

Rachael looked surprised. "I won't know what to buy unless you show me."

Dillon glanced toward the group of women again and saw that Thelma Bradberry, the biggest gossip monger in town, was among them. Her husband, Roy, practically lived at the Mustang. But he had beat Roy enough at cards to know the man would take great pleasure knowing there was a plain preacher lady sharing the ranch and would probably outdo his wife spreading the news inside the Mustang.

"Is something wrong, Mr. McKenzie?" Rachael asked when Dillon didn't speak after a moment.

"Everything is just dandy," Dillon muttered, turning for the grocery store. "If it got any better, I couldn't stand it."

The cooking lessons started as soon as Rachael unloaded the groceries, and Dillon had had time to check with Coot on the ranch work. "Okay, first I'm going to show you how to cut up a chicken," Dillon said, having decided that's what they would prepare for supper. Rachael, following his instructions, had already peeled potatoes and put them on to boil and opened a large can of baby peas.

"It's less expensive if you buy a whole chicken," Dillon said, pulling two whole fryers from the refrigerator. "I usually fry up two at a time so we have leftovers for lunch."

Rachael watched him tear open the plastic wrapper and marveled at the size of his hands. "Who taught you how to cook?" she asked.

He shrugged. "I just sort of picked it up, I guess. I've been doing it for as long as I can remember." He tossed the wrapper into the trash. "The first thing you need is a sharp knife . . ."

Rachael watched his hands, enjoying the lesson. She noticed that even though his hands were long and graceful, they were the hands of a man who worked hard for his living. They exuded power, and she knew the strength they possessed after having felt one enclose her wrist that morning. But something, instinct perhaps, told her those same hands could be gentle if he were so inclined. That thought warmed her insides.

"Did your mother teach you how to cut up a chicken?" she asked after a moment.

Dillon glanced up. "No, I learned from the men I lived with on various ranches."

"How old were you when you started doing ranch work?"

Dillon stood up straight, the butcher knife poised in midair. It amused him that she was no different from other women when it came to asking questions. He'd never met a women yet who couldn't fire them out faster than he could answer. "I left home when I was fifteen years old. I've been doing ranch work ever since."

"Where is your family?"

"Texas."

"Do you see them often?"

He sighed. "No. I get cards and letters once in a while, but that's about it." He arched one brow speculatively. "Now, is there anything else you want to know, or is this just an attempt to put off your cooking lesson?"

Rachael turned her attention back to the chicken as he resumed his work. "My mother wasn't very handy in the kitchen either," she said after a moment. "She died when I was too young to remember her, but my father used to tell me funny stories about her cooking antics." Rachael laughed shyly as Dillon glanced up briefly from his work. "I suppose it was lucky for both of us that my father was a gourmet cook."

Dillon processed the information as he carved the breasts expertly and laid them aside. Once he'd finished, he rinsed the pieces he'd cut and set them on a paper towel to dry. "You got any other family?" he asked.

"A couple of elderly aunts, but I was never close to them. They moved to Florida some years ago to get away from the cold weather."

It saddened Dillon that she had no one, although he couldn't imagine why. Perhaps it was because he didn't like to think of anyone being all alone in the world as he had been for so many years, as he still was. Or perhaps it was because he didn't want to feel responsible for her even though for some insane reason he did. Earlier that day when he'd refused to help her but had watched through the window as she'd resolutely entered one shop after another to introduce herself to the townspeople, he'd mentally thought, *Hold your head higher, Rachael. Look 'em straight in the eye when you speak. Stand straight.*

And those thoughts had confused him then as

they did now. He didn't want to worry about her. He didn't want to have to stand close to her and smell her scent, or gaze down into her expressive jewellike eyes, which she had never used to flirt or act coy the way most women he'd known had. He didn't want to take pleasure at the sight of her in that clean white apron, her pert nose lightly dusted with flour. Her freshness touched something deep in him, stirred a yearning that had never been filled as a child growing up in a house devoid of happiness, a craving that had never been met sharing bunkhouses with other men. The feelings frightened him, because they were so new and unexpected. Lastly, he did not want to be attracted to her because it would only complicate matters. He had no business noticing her legs or her cute behind or those high breasts. He preferred thinking of her as skinny rather than fashionably thin. He preferred seeing her as the plain-Jane type rather than a woman who was simply pretty in a natural way. He needed to keep reminding himself of these things.

Rachael couldn't help noticing the expressions running pell-mell across Dillon's face. "Is anything wrong?" she asked for the second time that day.

Dillon swallowed, and his Adam's apple bobbed painfully in his throat. "Everything's fine." But he knew something was indeed wrong. His thinking was out of whack. He squared his shoulders, clenched his jaw, and shut off the thoughts. "Your turn," he said, handing her the second chicken.

Rachael took the chicken he offered. Their gazes locked, and she wondered at the look there, wondered how he could look warm and friendly and approachable one moment, aloof and unyielding the next. She turned away, shook herself mentally, and fixed her attention on the bird in her hand.

Five

Over the next few days, Dillon taught Rachael how to prepare a meat loaf, a pot roast, and scramble eggs to doneness. Although she was an eager student, Rachael discovered she really wasn't very good in the kitchen and probably never would be. It wouldn't have been so difficult, she thought, if Dillon had taken the time to measure his ingredients properly so she could copy down the recipe. But with Dillon it was "a handful of this or a pinch of that," and with his hands being twice the size of hers, Rachael knew she would never get it right. She did, however, manage to get the taste of cleanser out of the coffeepot and learn how to use the old toaster.

On the third morning, Rachael handed Coot a small white box. "This belonged to my father," she said shyly when he looked up in surprise. "I cleaned it up and replaced the batteries. I hope you can use it." Coot opened the box and found a hearing aid inside. He blushed so badly that

Rachael was afraid she had insulted or embarrassed him. When she glanced up at Dillon in question, he muttered something about a job that needed doing and hurried out of the house.

Rachael rose at six every morning—now that she and Dillon had worked out a more realistic schedule—and once she'd dressed and prepared breakfast, she drove to the neighboring ranches and visited with the ranchers' wives for a while. The ranchers themselves were usually already hard at work on the property so Rachael used the time to get to know the women, staying for only a short while since they worked as hard as their husbands. Although the women seemed friendly enough, Rachael sensed a hesitancy about them and the old fear that they might ultimately reject her found its way back into her thoughts. Before leaving, she extended an invitation to services on Sunday.

"It will be very informal," she promised. "I've arranged to rent folding chairs from a store in Harley so we'll all have a place to sit."

In the evenings, with her chores completed for the day, Rachael worked on her sermon at the kitchen table. But by Saturday she was so nervous about presiding over her first service, she could barely sit still. Dillon noticed it when he came in to let her know he was going out for the evening.

"You're all wound up tonight," he said, grabbing a glass and filling it with milk from the refrigerator.

Rachael had put her foot down to his drinking right out of the milk carton, which was why he'd done it in the first place. Now he made a production of getting a clean glass each time and polishing it with his shirtsleeve before pouring from the sacred milk jug. It irritated her when he referred to the milk container as sacred, but once again, that's why he did it. Funny how in less than a week a man could learn to read a woman if he put his mind to it. Rachael might be a reverend, but she still had those funny moods and nit-picking qualities common to all women. This night, though, his efforts were totally lost on her.

"I'm just nervous about tomorrow," she said after a moment, tapping her pencil against the table as she spoke and trying not to notice how good Dillon looked. He was cleanly shaven, not a hair out of place, and his boots literally shone in the light. He was dressed for a night on the town, his jeans creased and his burgundy- and navy-striped shirt pressed neatly. Of course, it would never occur to him to thank her for ironing them, she thought dully.

"What's your sermon going to be about?" he asked, his curiosity getting the best of him. What did a woman like Rachael preach about? he wondered. Would she stand before his neighbors tomorrow and accuse them of being worthless sinners and make them feel guilty for whatever small pleasure they found in lives that were filled with so much hard work?

Rachael glanced down at the yellow legal pad before her. "I plan to speak on friendship."

Dillon arched one dark brow. "Friendship?"

"It's about people needing other people and being there for one another and that sort of thing."

"That doesn't sound like anything out of the Bible to me."

She tapped her pencil again. "I don't always take things directly from the Bible," she said. "I try to talk about what's important today. Like stress and illness and financial problems and relationships. Of course, I always back it up with scripture."

Dillon propped a fist on the table beside her and leaned against it. She looked comfortable and snug in an oversize knit sweater that brought out the blue in her eyes. Her hair, clean and shiny, hung free to her shoulders. Just looking at her, with her jean-clad legs tucked beneath her Indian-style on the chair, evoked cozy feelings inside of him. She was the kind of woman who inspired a man to kick off his boots and share the couch in front of a roaring fire, the kind of woman a man could snuggle up to and watch old westerns on television and drink hot chocolate with. So why was he going out into the cold to a place that would be crowded and noisy? he wondered.

Dillon grinned after a moment. "So what can you tell me about relationships, Reverend?" he asked. "I seem to be having a lot of trouble in that department these days."

Rachael grinned back in spite of herself. "I don't think we're talking about the same thing, Mr. McKenzie. You're obviously concerned about your relationships with women, but my sermon is about loving *everybody* because we need people in our lives and because love is an expression of God."

His grin broadened. "Oh, I'm interested in love," he said.

Now she knew they weren't talking about the same thing. "Then perhaps you'll come to services in the morning," she answered.

Still grinning, Dillon put the empty glass in the sink and stuffed his arms into his heavy jacket. "Don't count on it, Reverend. If I recall correctly, the Bible says a man is supposed to rest on

Sunday, and I plan to sleep till noon. G'night." He saluted her, turned on his heels, and hurried out. A moment later, Rachael heard his motorcycle churning down the long drive.

Rachael worked on her sermon until close to midnight, not because she didn't have it right but because she was too wound up to sleep. Her thoughts constantly strayed to Dillon, and she wondered . . . And then she told herself she had no right to wonder who he was with and what he was doing. She tried to convince herself that she was merely concerned about his soul and the effect his wild lifestyle might have on it, and that she was right to worry because it was her job.

But that was hogwash, and she knew it.

She could pretend all she wanted that her concerns were strictly professional, but she knew there was more to it. She was jealous because she suspected Dillon McKenzie was probably cozied up to a woman in some dark corner planning to do heaven knew what to her before the night was over.

Rachael squeezed her eyes tightly closed at the thought. She didn't want to think of Dillon McKenzie holding a woman in his arms—a sultry blonde with pouting red lips or a raven-haired beauty with generous curves, or a flaming redhead with a promise in her eyes. Rachael Caitland was jealous because she was none of those things. She was plain and thin and couldn't charm a man if her life depended on it.

Her experience with the opposite sex had been limited to a seminary student whose kisses had held about as much appeal to her as flypaper. Yet, she had imagined herself in love for a brief time, simply because she had never been in love before and didn't know any better. Nevertheless, she wasn't surprised nor overly disappointed when the man had developed a sudden interest in the pretty freshman in their Religious History class. Although she had envied their blooming relationship for a time and blamed herself for not being woman enough to elicit that same passion from him, Rachael realized there simply hadn't existed the sparks and closeness that were so important in a lasting relationship. Her experience in seminary and real life situations had taught her how important those sparks were, how they often paved the road to genuine love and strengthened the bonds of marriage.

And Rachael knew, deep in her heart where she housed her strongest convictions, that she had felt those sparks when Dillon McKenzie had kissed her.

She jumped in her chair the minute the thought surfaced, realizing with a jolt of common sense that she had no business thinking of the man in that light. Dillon McKenzie was everything she preached against—irreverent, self-centered, irresponsible, and pleasure-seeking. What could she possibly have in common with a man who smoked like a chimney, drank like a river, and cursed like an angry truck driver? He gambled and picked up women and freely admitted a penchant for pornography. He was a contradiction to everything she believed in.

Rachael gathered her things together at the table and stood, her head high, her back ramrod stiff, and she marched up the stairs to her bedroom with the stalwartness of a temperance worker through a crowded saloon. It was sheer madness to hold any romantic notions about a man like Dillon McKenzie and entertain the idea that sparks had flown between them. What she'd felt during that kiss had nothing to do with undying love and commitment. She had simply enjoyed the kiss because, after all, she was human, and because Dillon McKenzie was such an expert at it.

She couldn't imagine how many women the skunk had practiced on!

Rachael took a hot bath, slipped into a fresh gown, and climbed into bed, determined to take her mind off the man who'd haunted her thoughts all evening. But sleep did not come. She tossed and turned and twisted the covers around her legs but could not get comfortable.

Finally, at two A.M., Rachael climbed out of bed. Her bedroom felt hot and stuffy, and she longed for fresh air. She had spent a lot of hours cleaning in the house that week, and she'd missed the outdoors. Without wasting another second, she pulled her blanket from the bed, wrapped it around her, and went downstairs. She didn't bother with her bathrobe, knowing it was too lightweight to offer any protection from the night air.

It was cold when she stepped out onto the front porch. The velvet sky glittered with stars, blinking back at her as though in welcome. It was magical and probably the most beautiful thing she had ever seen. She took a seat in one of the wooden rockers and hunkered more deeply into the folds of the wool blanket. Her thoughts automatically turned to Dillon, and she wondered how many nights he'd gazed at that same inky sky. Would he appreciate the quiet splendor of it all, interspersed with the gentle baying from the livestock, or would he crave the nightlife offered at the Mustang instead?

How long she sat there, Rachael didn't know, but the night was suddenly split with a rumbling sound, far off in the distance, so subtle at first that she thought she had imagined it. But as the sound got louder, she recognized it as Dillon's motorcycle. Dillon McKenzie was on his way home.

A single headlight pierced the darkness, floating up the long drive like a ghostly vision. As it came closer, Rachael could make out the driver and the shiny helmet on his head. She tightened the blanket around her and scrunched up into a tight ball in the rocker, tucking her toes inside the blanket for warmth. Dillon would not see her there on the front porch, she knew. He would pass the house and never know she had seen him come in or suspect she had been waiting up for him. Which she hadn't, of course.

But Dillon did not pass the house. Instead, he steered straight for it and pulled to a halt near the porch. His headlight caught her in its gold beam, and the surprised look on his face told her he'd spied her there in the rocker.

Dillon cut the engine, and once again the night was bathed in quiet. With one boot, he brought down the kickstand and climbed off, then pulled off his helmet and set it on the seat. He regarded her for a moment in silence.

"Kind of late for you to be up, ain't it, Reverend?" he said, slowly taking the steps to the porch.

"I couldn't sleep."

Dillon propped one foot on the top step and crossed his arms. His stance was almost cocky as he took in the sight of her, the blanket draped over her small, shivering frame. "You wouldn't be waiting up for me now, would you?" he asked. The thought that she might have been pleased him. He couldn't think of a soul who would have waited up to see if he made it in safely, not even Coot, who was his best friend.

The smug look on Dillon's face told Rachael he was just conceited enough to believe she *had* waited up for him. He would naturally assume she had nothing better to do than wait up for his grand return, which only reiterated the fact he found her dull and predictable and plain. "Don't be ridiculous," she said in clipped tones. "My bedroom felt stuffy."

Dillon grinned, his white teeth glittering in the moonlight. "Stuffy or lonely, Rachael?"

She stiffened. "I have to go in now," she said, coming out of the rocking chair with her blanket still intact. "Good night, Mr. McKenzie." She turned for the door. Dillon chuckled, a low, throaty sound that made her shiver. She turned. "What's so funny?"

Dillon stepped onto the porch, and the planks creaked beneath his boots. "You are," he said, his voice amused. "I think it's funny that you're running away from me."

"I'm not running."

"You're as jumpy as a treed coon tonight, Rachael," he said, coming to a halt beside her. "Why are you so uptight?"

She didn't like the fact that Dillon could read her so well, didn't like the way her name sounded on his lips—deep and husky and a little too intimate for her comfort. He could read her emotions almost as easily as her own father had been able to. The only difference was her father had known her all her life. Dillon McKenzie had known her only a week. She suddenly realized that separate living quarters had not protected her emotionally from him, had not kept him from moving in too close where it counted. They were not sleeping under the same roof, but they shared everything else. They ate and worked together and spent many of their leisure hours in the kitchen, her working on her sermon, him figuring ranch costs in a black ledger, her sipping hot tea, him drinking black coffee.

"I merely thought you would enjoy sitting out here on the porch alone," she said. "I know I've sort of taken over the place since I arrived, and that's not fair to you."

Dillon leaned against the screen door, blocking her entry into the house. "Why should I want to sit alone when I could have the pleasure of your company?" he asked.

Rachael couldn't help but wonder how much he'd had to drink. "Did you have a nice evening in town, Mr. McKenzie?" she inquired, sarcasm slipping into her voice. She tightened her grip on the door handle, but he didn't budge.

Dillon shrugged. "Nice enough, I suppose." He didn't want to discuss the evening. He'd lost his usual wad at the poker table. And when Alicia Bridges, the new divorcée in town, had shown up, he found he wasn't really interested. He was too concerned with the notion that he was an irresponsible slob for gambling his earnings away every Saturday night. What kind of man was he? What kind of man would he become if he continued this lifestyle? Images of his father floated through his mind, but he shoved them away quickly.

"I reckon you think I'm some kind of heathen for

staying out in a bar half the night," he said after a moment, studying her profile in the dark.

Rachael leveled her gaze on him. "I try not to judge others too harshly, Mr. McKenzie, lest I be judged myself."

This brought a husky laugh from Dillon. "What could you possibly do, Rachael, that would cause others to judge you harshly?"

"I have my faults, Mr. McKenzie, just like everybody else."

"Yeah?" He looked greatly amused at the thought. "You ever slept with somebody, then wished you'd remembered to ask their name beforehand?"

Rachael was thankful it was dark and he couldn't see the blush his comment had brought on. Her palm felt damp against the door handle. "No, I haven't." She sniffed. "I would think that practice could be dangerous in this day and time."

"I was younger then and took chances, I suppose. Fear makes a man think twice before—" He paused. "Well, you know."

Rachael did not want to pursue the conversation. "I really have to go in now."

"You ever been in love, Rachael?"

The question surprised her. Rachael stared at him for a moment with her mouth agape. A cold breeze wafted across the front porch and caught her hair in its grip. It fluttered around her face. Dillon reached up and brushed it away, but his hand lingered. He took a thick strand and rubbed it between his fingers, and Rachael, staring back in mute wonder, was powerless to stop him. "I thought I was in love once," she finally said.

"What happened?"

His voice was like liquid velvet in her ear, inspiring confidence and coaxing an answer from her. "He didn't reciprocate. I realized I was wasting my time." She paused and laughed self-consciously, wondering what kind of game Dillon was playing with her. He was much too close for her liking. She could smell his woodsy after-shave. "But then I really wasn't surprised. I know what I am." Rachael regretted her words the minute she said them. Now, what had made her go and confess such a thing to Dillon McKenzie?

Dillon looked surprised. "What are you?"

Rachael dropped her gaze, letting it ride on his chest. "I'm not beautiful," she said with an indifferent shrug. "Actually, I'm plain."

Dillon pondered it. He released the strand of hair and lay his palm against her face, needing to feel the flawless skin that he had noticed the first time he'd laid eyes on her. He marveled at its smoothness, brushing his thumb across one silken cheek. "I don't think you're so plain, Rachael," he said. "You've got the nicest skin I've ever seen on a woman. And your eyes . . ." He paused. "Hell, they sparkle like Christmas tree ornaments."

Yes, the man was either drunk or out of his mind. Rachael laughed nervously and shook her head, but his hand remained steadfast at her cheek. "Mr. McKenzie, please. You're embarrassing me." But she could not help but enjoy the warmth of that same hand against her face, and she leaned into it, needing to feel that warmth and the nurturing his touch evoked.

"And your hair reminds me of a silky curtain. It's always so clean looking and smells like—" He thought about it. "Like those little wildflowers that come out every spring and make the air so sweet.

I'd like to see your hair fanned out on my pillow, Rachael."

Rachael gasped at his words and the images that filled her mind with split-second speed and clarity. She had enjoyed his touch but realized now they had gone too far.

"Does that shock you, Rachael?" he asked.

"Yes, Mr. McKenzie," she said, pulling her head away from his open palm. "Very much so, and I think it's time—" Her words died in her throat as he stepped closer.

"If that shocks you, then this is going to blow your mind." He'd barely gotten the words out of his mouth before he captured her in his arms and pulled her close. There was another brief gasp from her lips, but he caught it with his own, planting his mouth firmly against hers, kissing her, finally, after having wanted to since he'd seen her sitting there in the dark. She went dead still in his arms, and he knew with some sense of male satisfaction that he had indeed shocked her.

Rachael stood motionless as Dillon's lips made contact with her own, lips that were full and warm and tasted wonderful, lips that coaxed her own wide open for his eager tongue. Rachael's knees trembled, and she swayed against him, grasping his coat to keep from falling. Her blanket fell open, and Dillon slipped his hands inside.

A low rumble sounded deep in Dillon's chest as his hands, raw and cold from his ride home, found her heat. She was warm and soft and sweet. Her gown was smooth and silky, not at all what he'd imagined she wore those nights he'd stared up at her bedroom window from the bunkhouse. He gathered the material in his fists and rubbed it back and forth, chafing the skin beneath it that he knew would be as smooth as silk. Her mouth was like nothing he'd ever tasted before. It reminded him of nice things—fresh strawberries, dew-kissed peaches clinging to the tree. He thought of how she looked each morning when he entered the warm kitchen; fresh-faced and smiling, the white apron tied at her trim waist, making him forget the frozen ground and gray sky outside. He thought of her long legs, and knew her thighs would be equally nice. His big hands skimmed her waist now beneath her blanket and followed it downward where her hips swelled, and thoughts of her—innocent ones and not so innocent—culminated into desire, full and potent. He wanted her. That one thought filled his brain, choking out all others.

Rachael went stiff all over the minute Dillon's touch turned intimate, setting off an alarm somewhere deep in her dulled brain. Her lungs were on fire, near the verge of exploding, and her heart thundered beneath her breasts, sending her already-rapid pulse into a frenzy. She pulled away quickly, so quickly, she almost lost her balance. She breathed in, and the night air rushed into her lungs with a force that made her dizzy. She stumbled and blindly groped for the door handle. And she wondered, as she caught a glimpse of Dillon, how the man could look both amused and stunned at the same time?

"We need to get to bed now, Mr. McKenzie," she said, her voice sounding choked and alarmed in her own ears. She was trembling all over and couldn't think past wanting to escape him. Somehow, she had to get back to the safety of her room. Where she could breathe again and find rational thought.

"My thoughts exactly, Rachael," he said. "We *should* go to bed."

The way he said it told Rachael he wasn't thinking about separate beds. His words stunned her as much as his kiss had a moment before, stunned her more than the knowledge that she had enjoyed the kiss and would have preferred it go on. No man had ever lost his head over her or confessed a desire to sleep with her. The mere thought that Dillon McKenzie might want her shocked her beyond normal thought. Shocked her and sent a tiny thrill of anticipation through her body. But even as she let her mind ponder the possibility, even as she felt her belly warm at the thought, her lips formed a rebuttal.

Dillon covered her hand on the door handle once more. "You ever made love, Rachael?" he asked, surprising himself as much as her with the question. It was insane to ask her such a thing, and he knew it, but something more powerful than common sense seemed to be pushing him on.

"Mr. McKenzie—" Rachael wondered how things had managed to go so far. What power did this man have over her that she could fall into his arms so willingly? It was the same power that had led her out onto a cold porch to wait for him and know that he was home safely, the same power that made her worry that he wouldn't be warm enough on his bike at night, that his hands would chap without gloves. She squeezed her eyes closed again and tried to block out the handsome face and the voice that reminded her of thick honey lining a beehive.

"I'll bet you haven't," he said, ignoring her protest. "How can you run around talking about heaven when you've never let a man take you there?"

Rachael's eyes snapped open and her gaze collided with his. "Please don't insult me with blasphemy, Mr. McKenzie."

Dillon captured her hand. "And how come you call me Mr. McKenzie? Are you afraid to use my real name, Rachael?" He raised his hand to her face and touched her lips with a fingertip. "Say my name, Rachael. I want to *feel* you say it."

She felt as though she were being swallowed by everything around her, the night air, the flickering stars, Dillon's coaxing voice. The sensations filled her to the brink, and she gazed at the handsome face and knew she was lost to him.

"Dillon," she whispered against his finger.

He smiled. "I like the way you say it. I'd like to hear you whisper it in my ear and feel your body quiver and go slack beneath me."

It was too much. Rachael covered her ears with her hands and shook her head. "Stop this nonsense!" she all but shouted, and her voice startled them both and made her think more clearly. At his stunned look, Rachael reached for her blanket which had fallen off one shoulder. She pulled it tightly around her. "What do you think you're doing, Dillon McKenzie? Who do you think you are, coming on to me like this? You have no right." She didn't give him a chance to respond. "I don't know what you're after, but you've obviously come looking for it in the wrong place. I'd thank you to stay in town next time until you find it."

Her words hit Dillon like a wall of ice water, chilling him, yet forcing him to acknowledge with sickening clarity the words he'd spoken. What exactly *did* he think he was doing, he asked himself. He was suddenly embarrassed, embarrassed that he'd lost his head over a lady minister of all things, embarrassed that he was making a complete fool of himself in front of her. Anger and frustration surged through him, and he wanted to hit something. Better yet, he wanted someone to hit *him,* knock some sense into his thick skull.

"What makes you think I didn't find it in town, Rachael?" he asked coolly. He turned and made his way down the steps before she could answer, but not before he caught sight of the pain on her face.

Six

Coot was the only one present the next morning to hear Rachael's sermon. Standing at the window of the bunkhouse drinking his first cup of coffee for the day, Dillon couldn't help but notice how glaringly empty the driveway in front of the house was. And he could not help but feel sorry for the woman who'd labored so long over her sermon at the kitchen table each night in vain. Only a moment before, Coot had hurried out in his Sunday best—dark slacks, white dress shirt, and a faded green corduroy jacket.

"I'll save you a seat," he'd called out to Dillon before he'd closed the door behind him, before Dillon could tell him not to bother.

Dillon did not want to hear Rachael preach, did not want to hear her tell him what a worthless cuss he was. He'd never met a preacher yet who didn't try to drive that point straight home. And Rachael would surely feel that way after last night, after he'd more or less manhandled her on the front porch.

What could he have been thinking? he wondered not for the first time. He would never forget how still she had gone in his arms, as though shocked motionless by his actions. She'd probably been frightened out of her wits as well. And now, now that he'd gone and thrown himself at her, he didn't want to be reminded that she was a minister.

Dillon wondered what it was about Rachael that attracted him. He had certainly met prettier women. Not that Rachael wasn't attractive in her own right, but she was hardly the type a man would lose his head over or spin fantasies around. She was a reverend, for Pete's sake, a woman who'd already charted out a life of serving others. She would not welcome his groping hands on a dark front porch *or* his frantic kisses. And while she might discuss any spiritual or emotional difficulties a man had, he could not imagine she would be so eager to acknowledge his physical side.

Yes, he had lost his head, plain and simple, and he only had himself to blame. It'd had nothing to do with booze or an overt sexual desire, even though it would have been simpler to place the fault there. He'd done it out of curiosity and a yearning mostly, he supposed, mixed in with a lot of emotions he couldn't understand or put a name to.

He was falling for her, he thought suddenly, and that knowledge hit him with the force of a wrecking ball and almost made him spill his coffee. He was falling for a woman with whom he had almost nothing in common other than sharing a ranch. She was forbidden fruit, and he hungered for her in the worst way.

• • •

Rachael's smile looked as though it had been plucked from a ray of sunshine as Coot let himself in the front door, crumpled cowboy hat in hand, and made his way to the back row of folding chairs she'd set out earlier that morning. What furniture could be moved, had been, and the rest pushed flush against the wall.

"Good morning, Mr. Coot," she said, noting how his red hair had been slicked back with something that smelled like cheap cologne. The hearing aid she'd given him was tucked unobtrusively in one ear. Of course Rachael had no way of knowing it wasn't even turned on. "It looks as though we're going to have a small crowd this morning," she added, "but that just makes it all the more cozy. Don't you think?" She offered him another radiant smile, and nobody would have guessed she'd spent a sleepless night thinking of some cowboy and remembering his kisses. Nor would they have suspected how she'd spent the latter part of the morning nibbling dry toast and sipping tea to ease her nervous stomach when it was obvious she wasn't going to have a crowd at her services.

"Yes, ma'am," Coot finally said.

Rachael shuffled some papers unnecessarily at the small pedestal table that was to serve as her podium. "Will Mr. McKenzie be joining us this morning?" she asked.

Coot shifted in his seat. "I wouldn't count on it, ma'am."

Rachael sniffed, then covered her annoyance with another smile. "Then we can begin. Do you know the words to "Onward Christian Soldier,"

Mr. Coot?" she asked, passing him a mimeographed sheet of music.

Coot shook his head as he accepted it. " 'Fraid I'm not much of a singer, Reverend."

"Then I will sing for both of us, and you can help me with the chorus if you like. And then, when we're finished we'll talk a bit about the people that have meant most to us in our lives—"

"That would be Dillon," Coot offered.

"And how their love is a reflection of our Lord," she added.

"I'm afraid I don't see the resemblance, ma'am."

Rachael chuckled in spite of herself. "Then we've obviously got our job cut out for us, don't we, Mr. Coot?" He nodded and she went on. "And then when we break, we'll enjoy a nice Sunday dinner of ham and sweet potatoes that I put in the oven to bake first thing this morning."

Dillon studied Rachael surreptitiously over Sunday dinner, but if she was upset about the fact that Coot had been the only attendee at her service, she didn't give any indication. Nor did she make reference to the kiss they'd shared on the front porch the night before. In fact, she acted much the same as she always did, and that unnerved Dillon. Had she ranted and raved at him or treated him with aloofness, he would have at least known where he stood. As it was, he was left feeling confused and wary and more than a little uncomfortable.

Near the end of the meal, Rachael glanced up at Dillon and smiled. "Mr. McKenzie, I was wondering if you would give me directions to the old school building where my father used to preach?" she said. "I was thinking I might drive over this afternoon and have a look."

Dillon didn't quite meet her gaze. "I'll run you over in my truck later if you like."

"That really isn't necessary."

This time he did look at her. "You shouldn't go alone, Rachael. That building is old, and the floor is rotting in places. You could hurt yourself, and nobody would find you for days."

She nodded. "Then perhaps you won't mind driving me over once I get the dishes cleared away." He nodded and returned his attention to the meal and tried to do justice to the ham she had prepared per his instructions the night before. But he was too wound up to eat, and the tension between them was so thick, he felt he could reach out and grab it in his fist. He didn't like feeling so wired around her, he realized. He missed the easy camaraderie between them, the simple trust he'd learned to take for granted. He'd never had it growing up, which probably explained why he yearned for it so desperately now. He wanted to get past this unease which threatened their new relationship. But it wasn't that easy, he discovered.

He was aware of her every move, although he tried desperately not to be. He knew each time she blotted her lips with her napkin and how many times she raised her iced-tea glass to her lips. When she dropped her fork with a clatter, he jumped, then took pleasure in the fact that she was obviously as jittery as he was. What could be going on in her mind? he wondered.

It was the longest meal he'd ever sat through.

The school, a sagging frame structure that reminded Rachael of a tired old woman, was situated on the very edge of the ranch, tucked between a group of tall pines. Rachael and Dillon stepped through the double wooden doors and gazed at the main room, where the rows of empty desks looked rather forlorn with the sun barely streaming in through the tall, grime-covered windows. The chalkboard at the front was chipped and battered, and the whole room reeked of neglect. Rachael stepped forward.

"Watch your step," Dillon warned.

Rachael was thankful she'd changed out of her church clothes as she explored the building and found everything literally coated with dust. "So this is where my father preached as a young man," she said at last. She gazed at the front of the room. "You know, I can almost see him standing there as he would have looked back then."

"You and your father were close?" Dillon asked as he saw her expression soften, and knew a moment of intense envy for the man who'd meant so much to her. He couldn't help but wonder what it would feel like to be on the receiving end of that heartfelt expression.

She nodded. "Very close. Sometimes I wake up at night and forget he's gone, and I'll think of something I need to tell him and—" She paused and her blue eyes clouded. "Then I remember." She sighed and raised her eyes to Dillon. "Have you ever lost anyone close to you?"

Dillon shrugged. "Only Abel. But he and I fought like rattlesnakes, so I don't know if you'd call that close."

She pondered it. "Oh, I don't know. Sometimes it's the person who irritates us the most that we're closest to. We're afraid to face our true feelings so we fight to mask them."

Dillon chuckled. "Sounds like you're talking about you and me, Rachael."

"That's not what I meant," she said.

"But it makes sense, doesn't it?" He stepped closer and regarded her quietly for a moment. "Something happened between us the minute we laid eyes on each other, Rachael, and I think both of us have been doing everything in our power to deny it. At least I have."

"If we knock heads so often it's only because we're so different," she pointed out.

"But they say opposites attract, and I believe whoever said it knew what he was talking about. Either that or I'm losing my mind," he added reflectively, and glanced away. It had occurred to him more than once that he was indeed losing his mind. Why else would he be chasing after some prim and proper preacher lady who cared more about a man's soul than his libido?

Rachael thought Dillon looked almost vulnerable, but she knew him well enough to know he wouldn't appreciate the thought. "If you're talking about last night—" She paused. "You'll have to admit our emotions are running a bit high at the moment." When Dillon looked back at her, she went on. "I'm still mourning my father, Mr. McKenzie, and the fact I had to leave the church I'd come to love. And you, whether you believe it or not, have probably been somewhat affected by Mr. Pratt's death. "

Dillon knew he'd been saddened by Abel's passing. Although Abel had been ornery and the two had had their share of arguments, the old man had trusted him and treated him fairly. He knew deep in his heart that Abel had been the closest thing he'd ever had to a father, and when Abel had gotten sick it seemed only natural that he take care of the old man. He'd drawn an odd sense of satisfaction in doing so, he'd discovered, simply because it was the first time in his life anyone had truly needed him. In helping Abel, he'd helped himself. During those long nights and gray days preceding Abel's death, he had discovered his capacity to care.

Yet, Dillon could not imagine what Abel's death had to do with Rachael, and the turmoil he felt when he was with her. He had been saddened by Abel's death, yes, but had welcomed it when the man's pain had become so great, he could no longer enjoy life. True, he had cried for the first time in his life when Abel had simply stopped breathing, but he realized some of those tears had been shed out of relief.

Abel had touched him deeply by leaving him part of the ranch, he realized. He'd huddled in the cold on the front porch the day he'd left the attorney's office and silently thanked the old man who'd cared enough to provide for his future. Sure he'd cussed Abel under his breath from time to time for sending a lady preacher to share in the inheritance, but deep in his gut, he was thankful that Abel had remembered him, a common drifter who had nothing to show for his life.

But these emotions were separate from what he felt for Rachael. "You think you've got it all figured out, don't you, Rachael?" Dillon asked after a moment, amused that she, too, had obviously searched her own heart for reasons to justify their feelings.

"Not entirely, no."

He laughed softly. "But you think I kissed you last night because I miss Abel?" He didn't give her time to answer. "And you *let* me kiss you because you miss your father?" He leaned close, and his voice was edged with sarcasm when he spoke. "Yeah, right."

She stiffened. "I didn't really *let* you kiss me," she said. "I was just . . . taken by surprise."

"Which is why you went all soft in my arms and cozied up to me like—"

"Mr. McKenzie, please!"

"Oh stop with this Mr. McKenzie business, Rachael," he said sharply. "Don't you think it's a little late to stand on formality?"

"We should be going now," she said, walked toward the door.

Dillon didn't budge. "You're running again, Rachael. You do it every time we're together. Which only proves there's something going on here. But don't worry, it's scaring the hell out of me too."

Rachael paused at the door. When she faced him again, she was resigned. "Don't you think I know that, Dillon? I'm not stupid. And just because I'm a minister doesn't mean I don't have the same feelings and emotions as other women. People think since I carry around this title of reverend that I'm shielded against the emotions they have, but they're wrong. If anything, I feel things more strongly."

Dillon closed the distance between them. He halted only a couple of inches from her. "What do you feel for me, Rachael?"

Rachael's gaze didn't waver. "Mostly I'm confused."

"Why?"

This time her gaze faltered. "Because I'm somewhat attracted to you."

He grinned. "Just somewhat?"

She chanced a look at him. "Okay, very much attracted to you."

Dillon studied the porcelain face before him, and when he spoke this time, his voice was low and husky. "And what do you think about when you think of me, Rachael?"

His tone of voice and the way he said her name made her think of a lover's caress. "I think about the same things most women think of, I suppose. Last night I thought a lot about the way you kissed me." She wondered if she was being too honest with him. Surely a woman wasn't supposed to open her heart to a man so blatantly, especially when she had no way of knowing how he felt.

"And what did you think?"

Rachael swallowed. "I'm not very good at this, Dillon. I don't know the rules very well."

"Forget the rules, Rachael. They don't apply to us. Just give me the truth."

She sighed heavily. "I thought the kiss was good. Wonderful."

Dillon wanted to touch her but didn't, not because he didn't know she would feel good in his arms but because he, too, was confused.

"Did your thinking take you any further than mere kissing, Rachael?" he asked.

She dropped her gaze to his chest. "You know it did."

This time he did touch her, but not as he wanted. He simply cupped the back of her head in his hand and brought it to his chest. She didn't resist. How long he stood there, he didn't know, but after a moment the whole thought of what was going on made him laugh deep in his chest.

Rachael gazed up at him. "What's so funny?"

He didn't hesitate. "You and I. This whole situation. And the fact that I've never wanted a woman so badly in my life."

Rachael was even more confused.

"What does that mean exactly?"

"It means exactly what I said, Rachael," he answered. He crooked a finger beneath her chin and raised her face so that she had no choice but to look directly into his eyes. "I'm not going to give you a flowery speech about what I feel for you. But that doesn't stop me from wanting you, and if you were half-willing, I'd have you right here and now. And you can blush and be shocked and disgusted, but that's the way it is with me. I don't try to be something other than what I am."

"I'm shocked, Dillon, but not at you. I'm shocked at myself for wanting those same things."

Dillon sucked in his breath as her words hit home. "So what are we going to do about it?"

"What are we going to about it?" she echoed, then uttered a short, mirthless laugh. "We're going to go back to the ranch and forget we ever had this conversation, *that's* what we're going to do about it. Because I feel without a doubt it's a passing thing. I'm attracted to you because . . . well, because you're exceedingly handsome and I've never been in constant contact with a man. And I think whatever attraction you feel for me is simply because I'm unattainable."

"Unattainable?" He arched his brows in response. "Which means you don't think I have a snowball's chance in hell with you? That doesn't exactly bolster my ego, you know."

"Not because of any male and female thing but because of our extreme differences. It's not as simple with me, Dillon. I can't just fall for a man because he makes me itch in all the right places.

For me there has to be love and commitment and—"

"Marriage?" he said.

"All of those things."

Dillon pondered it. Of course she would expect all that, he thought. It didn't surprise him because he wouldn't have expected anything less from a woman such as her. She wasn't like some women who insisted they only wanted a good time with a man but sunk their claws into him and made for the altar the moment he got close enough. With Rachael, he didn't have to second-guess her motives. She was up-front and steadfast in her beliefs; the same today, tomorrow, and the day after. While some men might find it bordering on dull, he found it oddly comforting after living a drifter's life.

But he did not share her steadfast optimism about love and marriage and happily-ever-after. Life was not that simple for him. Sure he had his own place now, but he knew, even as much as he loved the ranch, he could bail out if it got to be too much. He was not one who planned for the future, because nobody, least of all him, knew what the future held. How could a man be expected to lock into a relationship and still be prepared to pick up and go at a moment's notice?

"You're right, Rachael," he said at last. "We need to go back to the ranch and forget we ever had this conversation. I must've been crazy to even think . . . otherwise," he added.

Rachael left the school building a moment later with Dillon at her side, and as she made her way to his truck, she wondered at the heaviness inside her. They had reached an understanding, and it was clear now that whatever they'd felt on the front porch was better left to rest. There would be nothing between the preacher lady and the rugged cowboy, and all those looks and secret thoughts that passed between them would be swept aside like dust. So why was she about to cry?

When Dillon and Coot stepped into the house a few days later, they found a two-year-old girl grasping Rachael's apron, and a baby in her arms, bawling as though his life depended on it. Both men took a step back.

"What's this?" Dillon demanded, gazing at the baby, who was doing his level best to gnaw off the plump fist in his mouth.

Rachael tried to talk over the noise. "Mrs. Cooper from Curly Q Ranch is flat on her back with the flu," she said, "and there wasn't a soul to help her with the babies."

"What about *Mister* Cooper?"

"His foreman quit on him without notice, so Mr. Cooper is struggling to do the work of two men at the moment." As Dillon's scowl darkened, she hurried on. "Of course, he plans to come by for the children at the end of the day, but for now there's no one to take care of them."

"Except you, right?"

Rachael was clearly surprised by his manner. "Does that bother you?"

Dillon yanked off his Stetson and tossed it onto a chair, while Coot took a seat at the table. He tried to cover his genuine concern for the family with brusqueness. And he didn't want Rachael to know he had a soft spot when it came to children. "Hell yeah, it bothers me. How do you plan to get your chores done around this place with those kids hanging on you?"

"I'll have to catch up with things after Mr. Cooper comes by, I suppose."

"And what are me and Coot supposed to do about our meals?" He shot an angry glance at what appeared to be the fixings for lunch, packaged cheese and bologna and a bag of potato chips. When he glanced back, he saw the baby had pulled the fist from his mouth and buried it in her thick hair, just as he'd wanted to do so many times. The little girl at her side jabbed her thumb in her mouth and pressed her face against Rachael's thigh, and for a moment he simply stared at the picture Rachael presented. He had never thought of her as having maternal instincts, but now he realized with her genuine love for other people, she would no doubt find children even more pleasurable. And he would have been blind to miss the way her expression softened each time she spoke to them. But he didn't want to think of Rachael in that light or wonder what she'd look like carrying a baby in her belly or nursing it or the million other things that sprang to mind. He searched for something to say, anything to put a stop to the flow of thoughts.

"And how come I spent the last week teaching you how to cook when this is all I can expect on the table when I come in after working my tail off all morning?" he said, pointing to the meager fare.

"I made it plain in the beginning that my church work comes first."

"Church work! This isn't church work, this is baby-sitting. Or are you so hard up for parishioners that you'll keep their kids and clean their homes as well?"

Rachael had had enough. "I do whatever is necessary to help people, Dillon McKenzie, and I don't much care what it entails. We also agreed on a little give-and-take around here, and you can't expect me to prepare a gourmet meal three times a day just because you think you have to have it."

Dillon snorted. "Lady, you couldn't prepare a gourmet meal if your life depended on it."

She sniffed. "Really, Dillon, you act as helpless as these children. I suggest if what I've prepared for you isn't suitable, you do it yourself. You're certainly able-bodied." She blushed as soon as she said it and hoped he hadn't taken it the wrong way. But the smug look he shot back told her he had indeed. "This is not the Stone Age," she sputtered. "Men cook and clean for themselves all the time."

"We had a deal, Rachael," he repeated, this time with less zeal. She was right, of course. He'd known all along where her priorities lay, and he was making an absolute fool of himself over it. But he would have bitten his tongue clean off before admitting it. That, and the fact he enjoyed hearing her say his name. At night, he sometimes imagined her whispering his name in his ears as she lay beneath him.

Rachael felt her temper flare at his obstinate look. "You have a choice, then. You can either eat your sandwich or . . . or starve." She turned on her heels and left the room, the baby still crying in her arms.

Coot chuckled as Dillon took a seat at the table and glared at the cold sandwich meat. "I think she means it, Dillon," he said. "If I were you, I'd shut up and eat."

"It's not right, Cooter," Dillon said, reaching for

the coffee cup next to his plate and hoping Rachael hadn't managed to mess that up as well. "That woman comes in this house, and the first thing you know she has taken over completely."

"You're right about that," Coot agreed, giving his friend a knowing look. "She has definitely taken over."

Seven

The following Sunday, Edwin Cooper and his two-year-old daughter joined Coot and Rachael for services. Before he left, Rachael handed him a chocolate cake she had wrapped for his wife who was still sick at home. He thanked her profusely on the front porch of the house as Dillon sauntered up and took a seat in one of the rockers. Rachael shot Dillon a dark look. His hair was mussed, he was unshaved, and he looked like the devil himself, grinning for all he was worth.

Dillon watched Edwin Cooper make his way to his pickup, and he chuckled at Rachael, who was still waving at the man from the steps. "You didn't tell Edwin you baked that cake now, did you, Reverend?" he asked her.

Rachael avoided his gaze. "He didn't ask, and I didn't volunteer the information."

Dillon lit a cigarette and blew out a puff of smoke. "Yeah, but you took the store wrapper off and wrapped it in aluminum foil to make him think you did."

Rachael sniffed. "So? What if I did? I didn't commit any great sin."

His dark eyes were amused. "No, but the little ones add up, Rachael, and before you know it, you'll be a fallen woman."

She sniffed again and opened the screen door to the house. "Dinner will be ready in half an hour," she said, and let the door slam behind her.

After a dinner of pot roast that Rachael had prepared almost single-handedly, Dillon announced he had to drive to the Lazy Eight Ranch to pick up a part for his tractor from Dan Holden, the owner, who also worked on tractors in his spare time. Rachael glanced up quickly.

"Would you mind if I rode out with you?" she asked. "I've been wanting to visit with Mr. and Mrs. Holden since I got here, but I didn't know how to get to their place."

Dillon frowned. "I really wasn't planning to hang around long, just to get the part and go."

"I won't be long. I promise."

Dillon sighed. "Yeah, okay, but I'm leaving in five minutes."

She smiled. "I can be ready in three." She still wore the neat cranberry dress she had put on before services that morning beneath her white apron, so all she had to do was run a brush through her hair. She was ready with time to spare.

Rachael tried to draw Dillon into conversation on the way to the Holden's ranch but getting information out of him was like trying to pull fresh meat from an alligator.

"How many children do Mr. and Mrs. Holden have?" she asked.

Dillon shrugged. "A houseful, that's all I know."

She nodded. She liked children. One day she hoped to have a Sunday school that would accommodate all the children in Jasper. "Dillon, I was wondering if you knew of any good contractors in the area," she said, changing the subject. "I've been wanting to meet with someone to discuss ideas for the church and—"

Dillon looked at her from across the seat of his truck. "You still planning to spend all that money on a church?"

His question sounded more like an accusation, and Rachael was surprised. "Of course I am. Why should I change my mind now?"

"Lord, Rachael, you don't even have a congregation."

She sniffed. "It's only a matter of time, Dillon, but when I *do* have a congregation I want them to have a decent place to worship. Not in somebody's living room with folding chairs. We need a place for the little ones to play, and a Sunday school class for the older ones," she added, voicing her previous thoughts.

"Not *we*, Rachael, *you*. What I need at the moment is a tractor that runs, but I won't spend the money because I don't know what to expect one day to the next, and I have to make sure I have enough money to make it. And here you are talking about building a fancy new church and—" He paused and shook his head. It was useless to try and make her understand. They had never been more divided. That's what made caring for her so frustrating.

"I never said it was going to be fancy," Rachael told him. "And you can't accuse me of being frivolous with the money Abel left, because I pinch pennies every time I get a chance." She sighed heavily. "But it wouldn't matter if I chewed them up first before spending them, because you'd still complain. Why don't you have a little faith?"

Dillon laughed out loud. "Faith! Is faith going to fix my tractor, Reverend? Is faith going to build that church you want so badly?" Was faith going to get him past wanting her.

"You're going to have to grow up and get your head out of the clouds before you can think of helping these people out here. You haven't lived through a winter and seen it kill half your livestock or been wiped out by a prairie fire or the million other things that can go wrong. Don't talk to me about faith, lady."

Rachael stared at him in indignation. "My head isn't in the clouds, and I don't appreciate your saying such a thing. I know how hard life is out here, I'm not entirely stupid. Or air-headed like most of the women you know," she muttered under her breath.

This amused Dillon. "What makes you think I go out with airheads?" he asked, deciding he'd had enough arguing for one day. Anyway, if Rachael wanted to blow every dime Abel had left her on a church, nothing he could say was going to stop her. She was a stubborn little cuss when she wanted to be, and he wondered if it had anything to do with the way she'd been treated by the members of her old church.

Rachael stared out the window. "I can't imagine a truly intelligent woman putting up with a man like you."

He chuckled. "What do you mean, a man like me?"

"Self-centered. Pleasure-seeking. Smug."

He arched both brows, but the smile never left his face. "Am I really all that, Reverend?"

"As well as a drinker and a gambler." She saw the smile fade from his face, and she regretted her words as soon as she said them. Her own face burned with shame. What right did she have to make such an accusation? But before she could apologize, he spoke.

"I'm not a drinker, Rachael," he said at last. "My father was, so I know the difference. I just let you believe that because I thought it would convince you to leave. But, yes, I do like to gamble now and then." He refused to look at her. "I need the thrill of high stakes or something, because I feel so dead inside sometimes." Dillon pressed his lips into a grim line. It was the first time in his life he'd ever admitted something so personal.

His confession surprised her as much as it did him, and Rachael didn't speak right away. "You didn't have to tell me that. I had no right to accuse you of being either."

"Then why did you?"

"Because when I look at you I see a man with so much potential, and I would hate to see it wasted and—" She paused.

"And?"

"I genuinely care what happens to you."

"Because of your role as a minister?" he asked quietly.

"No."

Dillon continued to drive. He hadn't gotten halfway to the Holden ranch before he realized he was humming an old country western tune he'd recently heard at the Mustang. Now, when had he become a humming man? he wondered.

• • •

Dillon followed Dan Holden to his toolshed and wondered if Rachael would honor the promise she'd made about only staying ten minutes. He'd never known a woman yet who didn't take all the time in the world when it came to talking and shopping.

"Is this what you want?" Holden asked, handing Dillon the tractor part he'd called about.

"Yeah, that ought to do it." Dillon took it and handed Dan a check. "I'm probably wasting my time because that old tractor isn't worth sending to a junkyard," he said.

"Why don't you break down and buy a new tractor and stop sinking money into one that's worthless," the other man said.

Dillon fingered the part in his hand. He wasn't one to confide in other people and certainly not about financial worries. Not that the ranch wasn't doing okay. But he had pulled it up from near bankruptcy once and wasn't about to risk it again. "We'll see," he finally said.

Holden regarded him. "You want a drink, McKenzie?" he offered, grinning. "I keep a bottle of Wild Turkey out here to keep me warm on cold days." He fumbled through some junk and came out with a pint-size bottle.

Dillon wasn't surprised to hear Dan hid booze out in his shed. He probably had a bottle hidden in the back of his pickup truck as well. It was a known fact that Dan Holden could put away more whiskey than six men combined, but that never stopped him from trying to prove it at the Mustang every time Saturday night rolled around. And it didn't stop him from climbing behind the wheel of his truck either when it was time to go home, although Dillon had tried to drive him on several occasions. That's the part Dillon had trouble with. If a man wanted to drink himself silly, that was *his* problem. But when he climbed behind the wheel of an automobile, it was somebody else's problem.

"No, I'm not in the mood, Dan."

The man nodded thoughtfully. "Aw, I get it. You don't want that preacher lady smelling it on your breath when you drive her back, huh?" Dan Holden unscrewed the top of the bottle as he spoke, then took a swig before replacing it.

Dillon shook his head. "I just had a big dinner." He sometimes wondered if Dan drank so much because he had an inferiority complex. Dan had never even completed fifth grade, and Ellen took care of the ranch business because Dan couldn't read. Folks that knew him better said it bothered Dan. Maybe drinking made him feel important, Dillon thought.

"So what's it like living with a preacher lady?" Dan asked as soon as he'd tucked the bottle out of sight.

Dillon shrugged and made his way out of the shed toward his truck. "We try to stay out of each other's way as much as we can."

Holden slapped him on the back and winked. "Yeah, sure you do."

Dillon came to an abrupt halt. "What's that supposed to mean?"

Dan offered him a sheepish grin. "Well, you know, the two of you all alone out there and all. I would think—"

"We have Coot with us," Dillon said quickly. "But it doesn't matter because she's not my type."

Holden threw back his head and laughed. "You

know what they say about a woman looking good as the night wears on," he said. "You might find the same holds true with preacher ladies way out there in the middle of nowhere."

Dillon felt his chest swell with anger. "I don't give a damn what *they* say, Dan. There's nothing going on between Rachael and me. And I'd thank you not to start some rumor to that effect."

Holden dropped his arm from Dillon's shoulder and took a step back. "Take it easy, old man, I was just kidding you."

"It's not a joking matter, Dan." He kicked his boot into the dust. "Are people talking about it?"

Holden coughed as though embarrassed. "Well, you know how some folks like to carry on. Especially that Bradberry woman. She mentioned to my wife in the grocery store yesterday that you had some preacher lady living out at your place."

"I moved into the bunkhouse as soon as she got there," Dillon said.

"I understand Abel left her half the ranch."

Dillon nodded, and the two walked to his truck. "I hope you won't let a little meaningless gossip stop you and your family from coming to Rachael's services," Dillon said, knowing he didn't want to be the cause if Rachael failed in her attempts to build a congregation. He'd seen how hard she'd worked. And he knew Dan's wife, Ellen, was a church-going woman.

The man laughed. "I'm not going to no church where there's a lady preacher anyhow, so don't worry about it."

"What have you got against lady preachers?" When Dan didn't answer right away, he went on. "You're the one who hired that ex-convict when nobody else would."

"Yeah, but that's different."

"Same thing as far as I'm concerned," Dillon said. "And if you shun the new preacher just 'cause she's a woman, folks out here are going to shun her too."

Dan frowned. "Why should they care one way or the other how I feel about the new preacher?"

"Because you've been around awhile and everybody respects you, that's why." Dan looked surprised, and Dillon went on. "'Course, I wouldn't want all that responsibility on *my* shoulders."

"What responsibility?"

"Well, by you staying away you might be keeping others away. It's sort of a slap in the face to the preacher lady that you'd rather drive to Harley for services than attend those right in Jasper."

Dan frowned. "What right do you have getting on my case? You don't attend the services either."

Dillon shrugged. "Yeah, but I don't have to worry about setting an example."

Dan was still frowning when Rachael came out of the house a few minutes later with Ellen Holden. He doffed his hat the minute they stepped closer. "Thank you for coming by, Reverend," he said. "I'm much obliged to you."

Rachael nodded and shook the hand he offered. "I'm only sorry I didn't get the chance to visit with you before I left," she began, then looked at Dillon and smiled, "but I promised Mr. McKenzie I would only take ten minutes." Dillon opened the door to the truck to help her in.

"Yes, well, maybe next time, then," Dan told her. "In the meantime, you can look for me and Ellen in church next Sunday."

Rachael as so surprised by the remark, she lost her footing and would have slipped had Dillon not been there to catch her. She had just spent the last ten minutes listening to Ellen Holden tell her that although it was nothing personal, she was not certain her husband would feel comfortable attending a church with a female minister.

"I look forward to seeing you, then, Mr. Holden," Rachael said once she'd gathered her composure, but she didn't miss the amused look in Dillon's eyes when she finally climbed into the truck.

The branding started a couple of weeks later, on a brisk day in April. For three nights, Rachael and Dillon had cooked. The night before the branding was to begin, they'd taken everything out of the freezer to thaw, and now, Rachael had it all heated. Coot came into the house promptly at eleven to help her load the food into the pickup so they could deliver it near the branding corral, and Rachael was ready, having boxed everything they would need.

They arrived a few minutes later and set up on the back of the truck where Rachael had draped several clean white tablecloths.

"Come and get it," Coot called out loudly, and was answered by a hearty cheer from the cowboys who'd been hard at work since five that morning.

Dillon was the first to arrive, looking hot and tired and slightly worried. "Is everything okay?" he asked.

"Fine. I packed enough food for the entire county."

Dillon nodded and gazed at the food appreciatively. There was fried chicken and pork chops and cold roast beef, potato salad and baked beans and a green-bean salad that he and Rachael had experimented on, not to mention a pan of homemade biscuits they had struggled over to get just right. And to top it all off, was a store-bought cake that Rachael had wrapped in aluminum foil. He grinned when he saw it.

The cowboys and ranchers were starved, and Rachael didn't disappoint them with the fare, piling their plates high and insisting some of them take a second plate to hold everything. She poured glasses of iced tea into tall Styrofoam cups and passed them out while the men searched for a comfortable place to sit. They didn't hesitate to get started, all of them chowing down as though they hadn't seen food in weeks. Rachael stepped forward shyly.

"Excuse me," she called out, and waited until the men had stopped talking. "Perhaps you'll pause just a moment so I can say grace."

The men swallowed, exchanged embarrassed looks, but bowed their heads just the same, a few of them even remembering to take off their hats. Only Dillon and Coot didn't look surprised.

When all was quiet, Rachael cleared her throat. "Heavenly Father, thank you for these good neighbors who have come together during this time to offer their assistance. Please bless their labors so they can continue the branding until all our neighbors have been taken care of." She paused briefly. "And please keep them free from injury, not only today but Sunday as well, so they can make it to church on time. Amen."

There was a chuckle among the cowboys, and when they looked up, Rachael offered them a hearty wink. "Enjoy your lunch," she said, and went back to work.

Dillon and Coot were late coming in for supper

that night, but Rachael kept the food warm. When they finally did show up, both men looked exhausted, and Coot had a case of the sniffles that sent Rachael scurrying to the medicine cabinet. But while serving dinner, Rachael noticed the worried frown on Dillon's face. "Did everything go okay today?" she asked.

He nodded. "One of the calves got away from its mother during the branding, though, and I'm worried. The calf is new and could get sick or die in the cold night air. But Coot and I have searched all over the place."

"We can go back out after dinner," Coot offered.

"Naw, you've done enough for one day, and you sound as if you're getting one of those spring colds you always get. Just try to get your rest tonight. I'll go out after I eat."

"I'll go with you," Rachael said. "I could hold the flashlight for you while you drive."

Dillon offered her a slight smile. "Thanks."

They searched for more than an hour, driving through pastures in Dillon's pickup truck while Rachael shined the light out the window, and Rachael couldn't help but be impressed that Dillon was so concerned about one calf when he had such a large number of livestock to worry about. But she had seen the careful records Dillon kept on the animals, had witnessed firsthand that day how he did everything in his power to make the castration and dehorning process as painless as possible.

"Doesn't that hurt him?" she had asked, knowing it was a stupid question but unable to conceal the fact that it bothered her so. She'd realized then that there were some aspects of ranch life she didn't want any part of.

Dillon, dirty and sweaty from his work, had

answered, "Hell yeah, it hurts. But my job is to see that it's done quick and neat. It's when a man gets sloppy that these poor animals suffer so badly, and there's no excuse for that."

He'd dismissed her then, going back to his work. Rachael had watched for a long time as he'd dealt with each animal quickly and expertly but not without compassion. She could see it on his face, hear it in his voice when he talked to them, and she'd known at that moment that somehow she had fallen in love with him.

She thought about it now as she rode with Dillon in his truck, feeling closer to him because of what she'd seen that day. Dillon had done everything in his power to make her think the worst of him, but she had found goodness in him despite it all. "Wait a minute," she said, and he stepped on the brake. "I thought I saw something over there in the shadows. Near those pine trees." Dillon slammed the gears into reverse and backed up while Rachael aimed the light toward the trees and brush. "Something moved," she said.

Dillon cut the engine and climbed out of the truck. "Be careful," Rachael told him. "It could be one of those coyotes you warned me about." But when Dillon glanced around at her, he found her smiling.

He found the calf standing near one of the trees, just standing there as though he'd been waiting for someone to come and get him. He cried out pitifully when he saw Dillon, and Dillon was glad now he'd made the effort to look. Rachael, who'd jumped out of the truck in the meantime, opened the tailgate so he could heave the calf up into the back, reassuring the scared animal in a low, soothing voice.

"I'm touched," Rachael said, gazing from Dillon to the calf.

Dillon slammed the tailgate. "Why?"

"That you care so much for your livestock."

"Does that surprise you?" He cupped his hands over the tailgate and regarded her.

She laughed softly. "Well, sometimes you try to come off sounding hard. Like the Big Bad Wolf or something," she added. "Sort of gruff."

"No, Rachael. If I were the Big Bad Wolf, I would have already made off with the goodies. The goodies being you," he added with a tired smile.

She blushed. "Oh."

He gazed up at the stars and sighed, and the sound seemed to come from his very soul. "But I've learned a lot about myself since you've been here. I've learned a man sometimes has to be patient where a woman is concerned. He faced her. "And I have been patient, Rachael, for as long as I intend to."

She blinked. "I'm not sure what you're talking about." She wasn't sure she wanted to hear it.

"I'm talking about you and me and what we're going to do now that we've found ourselves in this predicament. Living together but not really sharing a life." When she started to speak, he put a finger to her mouth and hushed her. "The last time we had this talk, you told me we should go back to the ranch and forget everything that was said and try to ignore the attraction between us. At first I thought it was a good idea." He moved his finger and shook his head. "But it's not working."

"Perhaps we're not trying hard enough."

"It's not *going* to work, Rachael," he said, "and do you know why?" She merely shook her head, not trusting herself to speak. "Because every day I see you," he said. "Next to Coot's ugly face, you're the first thing I see in the morning and the last thing I see at the end of the day. I've seen your good moods and your bad ones. I've seen you at your worst, pacing the floor on a Saturday night while you're putting the finishing touches on your sermon and snapping my head off when I disturb you, and I've seen you at your best, doing small things for Coot that please him so much."

Rachael smiled. "Yes, well, we do spend a lot of time together, and I know I get in your hair. But I plan to start doing things, getting out of the house once in a while now that the place is settled."

"That's not what I was trying to suggest, Rachael," Dillon said, watching the way the breeze fluttered through her hair. He reached for a strand and fingered it. "I was trying to suggest we spend *more* time together." He took a deep breath before he added, "As man and wife."

Eight

For a moment Rachael stood there and stared and thought she must have misunderstood him. And she couldn't think what he could have possibly said that would have come out sounding like the words *man* and *wife*. *Land* and *strife*, she thought, playing a little word game with herself as she continued to stare, a frown playing at her brow. Finally, she laughed.

"You're not going to believe what I thought you said."

"I said it, Rachael, believe me. As many times as I've practiced it the last couple of days, there's no way I could have gotten it wrong. I asked you to be my wife."

"But Dillon!"

"And before you start thinking of a million reason why you shouldn't, I want to give you some reasons why you should."

"But you don't love me," she said matter-of-factly, then held her breath as she waited for him to reply. And there was a part of her that wished he would deny it, simply because she would then feel more comfortable about admitting her own feelings for him. What had started out as a few sparks had blossomed into love in just a matter of weeks. And that thought frightened her to such an extent that she shoved it aside every time it entered her mind.

"I'm not sure I know what love is," Dillon confessed after a minute, "and I've only used the word when I had to." He glanced away. "Some women like to hear it whether a man means it or not." He focused his gaze on her once more. "But I'll say it if that's what it takes."

She didn't hesitate. "No. I don't want false promises, Dillon. I've always been honest with people, and I expect the same."

"Come here, Rachael," he said, and reached for her. She didn't protest as he slipped his arms around her waist. "That doesn't mean I don't care for you, because I do, and that's a lot coming from me. I've never really given a damn about anybody in my life. I never stayed in one place long enough to build any kind of relationship. Coot and Abel were the first real friends I ever had." He smiled softly as her look turned incredulous. "You've touched something deep inside of me, Rachael. You've wakened up a part of me that I didn't know existed. I'm a better man when I'm with you." He paused. "All I know is, it *feels* right when we're together."

She fumbled for a reply. "I'm not sure that's reason enough to get married, Dillon, and I'm not really sure I would make a good wife. My work is important to me, it's more than a job. And I would never want to disappoint you."

"How could you?"

"I'm not experienced with some things as you must know. And I'm probably not as pretty as most women you've been around."

"You're the most beautiful woman I've ever laid eyes on, Rachael Caitland," he said with conviction. "Your eyes light up a room like a thousand bulbs, and I can't tell you how many times I've wanted to touch your skin. All of it," he added, and felt her shiver in his arms.

"I'm thin," she protested, then quickly added, "but I've gained four pounds since the cooking lessons began."

He chuckled and hugged her against him. "Which means I won't have to put up with a fat wife like some of the ranchers." He paused and gazed at her thoughtfully. "You'll put on weight once the babies come."

Babies. Rachael shivered again and laughed to hide the bright blush on her cheeks. "You talk as if I'm one of your heifers, Dillon. A man and woman should be deeply in love when they marry. They shouldn't make that sort of decision simply because it's convenient and fits in with their plans. You're not doing this to have more control of the ranch, are you? Because if it means that much to you, I would probably sign over my share." She realized as she said it that it was extreme, but so was his suggestion of marriage. Yet, she knew in her heart she would do it, to make him happy. Ranching was his lifeblood, and Dillon was responsible for its success, not her. He deserved full ownership. "I mainly care about building the church," she said after a moment.

Dillon didn't quite know what to say. He was touched to the core by her offer. Had she told him

that in the beginning, he would have been ec-
static. Now it wasn't as important. The only thing
that was important was knowing Rachael cared.
Nobody had ever cared that much.

"That's not what this is about, Rachael. And as
far as love, I think I can guarantee it will happen
for us. We already care for each other and respect
each other. For now, what we have should be
enough."

But Rachael already knew she was in love with
him. She hitched her head high. "If I were your
wife, I wouldn't appreciate your spending Saturday nights at the Mustang."

He grinned and kissed her on the tip of her nose.
"I'm counting on that, lady. It's a hard way to live,
but I never knew any other way before you came
along." He paused and his eyes caressed her face.
"You've filled a need in me that I've never been able
to find at the Mustang or places similar. Marry me,
Rachael, and give me all those things, the stability
I've always craved. You'll be saving me from myself,
you know."

It was too much too soon. "I'll have to think
about it."

"You mean pray about it?"

"Yes."

Dillon winced at the thought of her going down
on her knees before the Man upstairs to inquire
about a man such as him. After a moment,
though, he grinned. "Okay, but kiss me first so I'll
have a little leverage."

Rachael raised her lips to his and closed her
eyes. He captured them but a second later raised
his head slightly. "Kiss me back, Rachael," he
ordered against her tight-lipped mouth. "Just let
go for once in your life."

This time when Dillon touched her lips, they parted slightly, and he slipped his tongue inside and found what lay beyond. He drew her closer, fitting her soft curves against the hard planes of his body, and something male in him rejoiced at the intimate contact. But he kept himself in check at all times, even as he sought her own shy tongue and bonded with it. He would be patient a little longer, knowing that by rushing her he might scare her off. Rachael was different from any women he'd ever known. With Rachael, he had to deal in emotions. But soon, very soon, he meant to have her. She was no longer forbidden fruit; she could give him life.

Rachael spent another sleepless night in her bedroom thinking of Dillon's marriage proposal. At first it was too impossible to consider. Not that she hadn't thought of getting married one day. In her mind she had seen the kind of man she would eventually marry—gentle, caring, sensitive, a man who was just as devoted to serving the Lord as she. A man who understood suffering and simple human need. She and her husband would have children, of course. In her dreams, she saw little boys in blue sailor suits, and daughters in white frilly dresses—who would all share the front pew in church and carry little white Bibles engraved with their names. Afterward, they would go home and have Sunday dinner that their father had prepared and take long walks together. It sounded perfect at the time.

Now it sounded boring.

True, she wanted a man who was gentle and sensitive, but she also wanted a man who was strong and aggressive and—Yes, she wanted a man who was a little bit cocky too. And while she wanted someone who shared common goals with her, she didn't want a namby-pamby relationship where there was no struggle or conflict and very little to get excited about. She wanted a man who looked beyond a person's exterior and found goodness and beauty inside, but at the same time she wanted a man who would appreciate her as a woman as well, and maybe even buy her sexy lingerie once in a while. Simply put, she wanted sparks when a man kissed her, not flypaper. She wanted a man who could make her burn.

Rachael blushed as soon as the thought surfaced. Now, where had that come from! But it was true, she told herself. She wanted someone with whom she could experience all her emotions. She liked it when Dillon teased her or made off-color remarks that sent her stomach fluttering. And she liked the little tremor of excitement that pulsed through her veins whenever he so much as brushed past her in the kitchen, and the way her insides softened like warm chocolate when he kissed her. Of course she would never admit it to him.

She looked forward to seeing him first thing in the morning, hunkered deep into his heavy jacket as he came in from the cold, his Stetson pulled low on his head. She had come to recognize his footsteps from Coot's, the sure, steady sound of his boots against the plank floor. She enjoyed listening to him talk to Coot about ranch business first thing in the morning over coffee, his voice low and lulling and intimate. And she enjoyed seeing him at the end of the day at supper, freshly showered and pleasantly tired, just as much as she enjoyed sharing the kitchen table with him once the chores were behind them.

Yes, she wanted these moments with Dillon McKenzie, despite their multileveled differences. She wanted the comfortable moments and those that were not so comfortable, those times when they simply didn't agree. She wanted the peaks and valleys and upheavals just as she wanted the flat, smooth-running surfaces in their relationship, knowing her life would be richer because of it. Yes, it was only right they should marry, she decided.

And she knew with enough love and patience and faith, she could turn Dillon McKenzie into the man he was destined to be.

When Dillon and Coot stepped into the kitchen the following morning, they found Rachael waiting for them, standing at the kitchen table with her hands folded demurely in front of her.

"Good morning," she said softly, and both men doffed their hats. "I have an announcement to make." When Dillon glanced at Coot uneasily, Rachael hurried on. "Dillon, I would like for Mr. Coot to hear this if you don't mind, since the three of us are so close." When Dillon reluctantly nodded, she went on. "Mr. Coot, Dillon has asked me to marry him, and I've decided to accept."

Rachael couldn't decide which man looked more surprised. Coot immediately slapped Dillon on the back and shook his hand. "Congratulations, old boy," he told him, then shook his head as though he still found it hard to believe. "I don't' know why I'm so surprised," he admitted. "It's not as if I didn't see it coming." He looked at Rachael, and his eyes softened. "Mind if I be the first to kiss the bride?" he asked.

Rachael laughed. "I would be sorely disappointed if you didn't, Mr. Coot." Once Coot kissed her, she noticed he wasn't wearing the hearing aid and pointed it out to him. "Has your hearing improved?" she asked.

Coot blushed so badly, his ears turned red, and he didn't quite meet her gaze when he spoke. "I reckon it must've been one of those miracles you so often preach about, Reverend."

Rachael and Dillon were married late one afternoon the following week at the church in Harley. Coot, their only attendant, served as best man. Dillon was so nervous, he had dry heaves beforehand, and Rachael was certain he would never get through the ceremony for sweating. Although she and Coot joked about it, she couldn't help but wonder if Dillon was having second thoughts. But when he kissed her after they'd been pronounced man and wife, all her doubts fled, and she was gloriously happy. Afterward, the three of them, upon Rachael's insistence that Coot go as well, had dinner at the best restaurant in Harley. Finally, Dillon seemed to relax a bit. The sun had already set when they made the drive home.

Then it was Rachael's turn to be nervous. Suddenly, it was all she could do to keep up with the lively banter going on around her. A smile frozen to her face, she watched Dillon turn off the main road and make the half-mile drive to the house. Once Dillon had parked and shut off the engine, Coot got out on the passenger's side and immediately and conveniently excused himself, congratulating them once more before he disappeared in the direction of the bunkhouse.

"Well, here we are," Rachael said, as soon as she had unlocked the front door of the house. She sighed and gazed anxiously at the man who was now her husband. He was dressed in a navy suit she had purchased for him the day before in Harley. He had grumbled, of course, but had worn it anyway, then told her to get a good look because it would be the last time she saw him in it. Rachael had smiled benevolently and pinned a carnation to his lapel.

"Yeah, here we are," Dillon echoed after a moment, still dazed at all that had occurred that day, not to mention the ones leading up to it. They'd rushed like mad to get a license so they could marry as soon as possible at his own insistence. He still couldn't believe she was his wife. "I suppose you're waiting for me to carry you over the threshold," he said dully when Rachael didn't make a move to go inside. He'd seen it done in the movies and had sworn he would never let a woman convince him to do such a damned fool thing. But, standing there gazing down at the wistful look on her face, he knew he would do it if it was important to her. Maybe it would help break the ice, make her relax a little, he thought.

"You don't have to do it if you don't want to," Rachael said, reading the resigned look on his face. She felt silly now for thinking he might. Theirs was not the usual run-of-the-mill marriage, and she would only be fooling herself to think he'd be eager to share the same traditions as other newlyweds. True, their marriage had been founded on trust and deep caring, but it also had a lot to do with comfort and necessity. Dillon McKenzie was not giddy over her.

As Dillon gazed down at Rachael, he wondered

when he had ever thought her plain. At the moment, she looked beautiful, her thick hair pulled back from her face with ivory combs. She was dressed in a white linen suit that he supposed she'd bought in town when she had purchased his suit, her wedding present to him. He felt a little guilty now that he hadn't gotten her anything or planned a honeymoon. But he hadn't wanted to spend the money or take time away from the ranch. And she hadn't pushed.

Looking down at her, Dillon grinned suddenly. "I didn't want to wear this suit either, but that didn't seem to bother you any."

Rachael laughed, and she stepped closer and reached to straighten the tie she'd selected for him. It felt nice to be about to touch him as she pleased—nice but strange and new. Perhaps by touching him now she would be less nervous later. Her fingers brushed his throat, and she almost shivered at the contact. "Yes, well, if you knew how handsome you looked in it, you'd wear it every day," she said. "Or at least to church on Sunday."

Dillon cocked his head to the side. He liked the feel of her hands on his body no matter how innocent. "I don't go to church, remember?"

She smiled, stood on tiptoe, and kissed him. "So I've noticed, cowboy."

Dillon stepped closer, until his thighs met hers, until her cheeks turned pink as a result. "But you think you're going to change all that, don't you, Reverend?" He shook his head, and his eyes told her it wasn't likely.

Rachael shrugged and cocked her own head to the side, trying not to let on how unnerved she was by his nearness. "Stranger things have happened."

Dillon's body responded immediately. Without

taking his eyes off her, he reached forward and lifted her high in his arms, no longer caring how foolish it looked or how silly he felt doing it. Once inside the house, he kicked the door closed with a single thrust of his hip. "Where to?" he asked, still holding her.

Rachael snaked her arms around his neck and snuggled against him. "Do you think you can carry me upstairs?" It was a bold thing to ask, she realized, but she felt it would be easier if they entered together and tried to get past their initial discomfort as soon as possible. Besides, it wasn't as if she hadn't tried to prepare herself for this moment.

He chuckled. "A skinny little thing like you?"

She slapped him playfully. "I'll have you know I've gained six pounds since I got here. If you keep making fun of me, I'm going to eat so much, you'll need a crane to lift me to the second floor."

Dillon took the stairs to the top floor and stepped inside the bedroom he would now share with her. With her help, he had moved his belongings in the night before. His Stetson sat on one end of the dresser, along with his brush and comb and several bottles of cologne. Her belongings were neatly lined up at the other end—perfume, a metal tin filled with potpourri, a silver-plated comb, brush, and mirror set, and a satin box of barrettes and hair bows, some of which had spilled out in her obvious haste to dress that afternoon.

Rachael saw that he was staring. "What are you looking at?" she asked, wrenching her neck around in the direction of his gaze.

He looked at her. "I guess I never really thought you liked pretty things."

"I love pretty things. I'm a woman, aren't I?"

He grinned. "I hope so." He carried her to the bed and lowered her onto it, then sat on the edge. He took one of her hands in his and studied it for a moment, noting the clean nails and smooth skin. Smooth, the same as the rest of her. "Maybe I'm rushing things," he said after a moment. "I mean, it was me who insisted we get married right away, but I never really thought past that point. Well, I *did* think past that point, but we never really discussed it," he amended quickly. He looked at her. "Maybe I should back off now, give you a chance to adjust to all this."

Rachael gazed up at him with her heart in her eyes. She saw need and desire written all over his face, and it touched her deeply that this handsome man, the same man who'd promised himself to her that very afternoon, wanted her. *Her*, plain Rachael Caitland from Sioux Falls who'd never even been asked to dance. Suddenly her love for him outweighed her nervousness. She smiled coyly, even though coy wasn't easy for her. "You wouldn't disappoint me on my wedding night, would you, Dillon?"

Nine

Rachael's words were so totally unexpected, so out of character for what he would have anticipated from a minister, that for a moment, Dillon wondered if he'd heard her right. He had wanted to give her time if she'd needed it, let *her* call the shots, and, *that*, he knew, was totally out of character for him. He had always been a little impatient where women were concerned, but he had promised himself he would not be with Rachael. He would give her time. He would share her bed and nothing more if she preferred, no matter what it cost him physically. But Rachael had just informed him that wouldn't be necessary.

All at once he grinned. "No, I'm not going to disappoint you, Rachael," he said, his eyes soft with promise.

She blushed in spite of herself, in spite of her decision to approach her wedding night with dignity and sophistication. Sophistication. She wanted to laugh. She had never made a sophisticated move in her life, and now she wondered what had made her think she could pull it off on this of all nights.

Rachael raised up from the bed, turning her head to one side slightly so he could not see the rosy flush on her cheeks. "I think I'll slip into something more comfortable, then," she said at last. "Would you excuse me?"

"Sure." Dillon jumped up so fast, he almost toppled the lamp on her night table. He caught it swiftly and muttered a four-letter word under his breath, mentally chiding himself for being so nervous. Rachael, climbing off the bed, giggled, and he shot her a dark look. She was still snickering as she hurried out of the room into the adjacent bathroom. Somehow, laughing seemed to help her nervousness, she noticed. But she couldn't imagine why Dillon was so anxious. Surely this sort of thing was old hat to him. She pushed the thought aside. She did not want to think of her husband's sexual experience on her wedding night.

Rachael's laughter died in her throat once she reached the bathroom and found her ivory satin chemise and wrap, the set she'd purchased in Harley, hanging on the back of the bathroom door. She fingered the material and wondered if Dillon would like it, wondered what other brides wore on their wedding nights.

Rachael stepped out of her linen suit and hung it neatly on a hanger, then began peeling away her panty hose and underclothes. It was the first time in her life she'd ever gone to bed without all her lingerie and night wear in its proper place. But then, she had never dressed for bed with a man in mind. That thought unnerved her so, she stuck a fingernail clear through one leg of her hose. She sighed and tossed them aside. Get a grip, she told herself.

Holding the chemise over her head, Rachael let it whisper down her arms in a caress, guiding her head through the opening at the top. And she thought of Dillon who would eventually remove it, Dillon whom she had fallen desperately in love with despite their differences. And she said a silent prayer for him, for herself, and their marriage, and blessed the miracle that had brought them together.

Dillon paced the bedroom like a caged animal, then realized how much noise his boots were making on the plank floor and removed them. He loosened his tie, then pulled it off completely and draped it on the back of a chair. His jacket followed. He stood for a moment and listened for sounds coming from the bathroom and wondered what could possibly be taking Rachael so long. Had she been any other woman, he would have stripped naked and climbed beneath the covers and that's where she would have found him, warm and hard and waiting. But this was *not* just any woman, this was Rachael, and he didn't have the slightest idea what to do next.

The bathroom door opened, and Dillon jumped. Rachael stepped into the room a second later wearing a short white satin wrap and looking for all the world like an angel. Dillon swallowed, taking in the long legs that had tempted him in the past. His gaze flickered over her appreciatively. Her hair, having been loosened from the combs, hung full and rich at her shoulders. Her eyes sparkled like sapphire in the lamplight. Dillon forgot his nervousness and went to her.

He touched her cheek. "You don't look like any

minister I've ever seen before," he said, smiling tenderly.

"I wasn't trying to look like a minister," she said, returning a smile of her own that was slightly tremulous but warmed his heart as surely as if he'd plucked it from his chest and hung it before a wood-burning stove. "I was trying to look like your wife." She paused and met his gaze. "I hope that's okay." Her voice sounded unsure in her own ears.

Dillon answered with a kiss, tipping his head forward until their lips touched. He brushed hers lightly with his own and gathered her into his arms, where she snuggled like a kitten come in from the cold. And he marveled at how good she felt, how *right*. Who would have suspected it, he wondered, a Bible-cartin' preacher and a rough-and-tumble cowboy?

Rachael slipped her arms around Dillon's neck and brought him even closer, parting her lips and inviting his ready tongue inside. The kiss deepened, and she felt her emotions swirl around her in a sensual fog. Rational thinking disappeared as her senses took over. She reveled in the touch and taste of his lips—full and firm and pleasantly scented. His hair was thick and coarse beneath her searching fingers, the back of his neck corded with muscle. She sank against his solid chest and knew she had come home. Her decision to marry him had been the correct one, and she realized she loved him and wanted him as much as she did her next breath. She kissed him with a fervor she had never shown.

This time Dillon did not have to be coaxed into lifting Rachael into his arms. Without breaking the kiss, he swept her up against his chest and carried her the short distance to the bed. He laid her down gently, then began the process of removing his clothes.

At first he was so self-conscious in front of her, he could barely manage to get his socks off his feet. He hopped on one foot for a moment as he peeled one sock away, glancing up every now and then at Rachael, who was trying her level best not to look at him. He didn't know which of them was more anxious. Finally, he stood straight and tossed the sock to the floor as though it were personally responsible for the turmoil he was feeling.

"Let's get something straight," he said tersely. "When we're in the bedroom, you are no longer a minister."

"Okay." So that was the problem, she thought.

"You are simply my wife."

"Yes." She nodded enthusiastically.

All at once, Dillon found himself laughing, loud, hearty guffaws that shook his broad shoulders. He relaxed. "Damned if this isn't the most unusual situation I've ever found myself in," he said, "trying to romance a minister."

"I'm sorry, sweetheart."

Sweetheart! Dillon unbuttoned his shirt and shrugged out of it. Nobody had ever called him that in his life. He tossed his shirt onto the chair and reached for the fastening to his slacks. He undid it, shoved the pants past his knees, and stepped out of them. He did the same with his underwear. When he was finally completely naked, he met Rachael's eyes.

She didn't speak right away. She stared for so long that Dillon couldn't help but wonder at her blatant but almost childlike curiosity. He shifted uncomfortably under her gaze but didn't make a move to go to her, simply because he wanted to give her time to acquaint herself with his body.

Rachael drank in the sight of him, the enormous hair-roughened chest, the nubby brown nipples that appeared erect in the light. It was not the first time she'd seen his chest, but it was the first time she had felt privileged to study it. She lowered her gaze to his flat stomach where the hair grew sparse and followed the black hairline to the thatch where his sex nested. His thighs and legs appeared as strong and powerful as the rest of him.

Rachael's gaze climbed the length of him and locked with his puzzled one. "You are a magnificent man, Dillon," she said after a moment. "I am lucky to be married to you." She held out her arms to receive him.

She said it so sincerely that Dillon was genuinely touched. He went to her, climbing beneath the crisp, sweet-smelling sheets where she waited, warm and soft and fresh as spring flowers. He kissed her deeply, cupping her head in his palms as he explored her mouth with his tongue. He broke the kiss, and his lips reappeared at her closed eyelids, brushing them as gently as a night breeze playing across the prairie. He kissed her temples, her throat, and finally dipped his tongue inside the shell of her ear. A delicious shiver racked her body, and Rachael laughed self-consciously.

"I've never had anyone do that to me before," she confessed in a whisper.

"We're going to have to change all that, aren't we?" he whispered back, readjusting himself so that she was not bearing the full brunt of his weight. And then, as he recaptured her lips, Dillon sought out the belt of her wrap and untied it. Once he'd pulled the knot free, she assisted him by shrugging out of it. Her short gown was next. He lifted it over her head and tossed it aside.

Dillon sucked his breath in sharply as he gazed down at the woman before him whose skin looked almost translucent under the glow of the lamp. Her breasts were small, tipped with coral-shaded nipples that enticed him beyond rational thought. His gaze moved past her trim waist and hips to the brown tuft of curls between her thighs, and he could not resist touching her any longer, stroking those creamy thighs and toying with the hair that covered her femininity. Rachael gasped, surprised and delighted with his bold touch. "You're beautiful, Rachael," he said sincerely.

He captured her lips once more and kissed her, lingeringly, before moving to her breasts. Once there, he paid reverent homage, cupping them with his palms, wetting them with an eager tongue. He fit his lips around one nipple and tugged, and Rachael felt the sensation deep inside her womb.

She arched against him, the last shreds of shyness melting away like sunlight in a dusk sky, replaced with something more potent and powerful than mere timidity. Kissing her once more, Dillon moved one hand between her thighs, and Rachael moaned softly as desire sprang to life, a coiling heat that filled her with as much anxiety as it did pleasure. A second later, she felt Dillon's exploring fingers searching past the folds that housed her secrets. And then he found what he was looking for—an elusive bud, so erect, so sensitive that she shuddered at the contact. He played with it, toyed with it, until Rachael found herself gasping for her next breath. He dipped his fingers inside, and she blushed at the honeyed warmth that greeted him.

"It's supposed to be like that," he said, noting her discomfort. "Don't be embarrassed."

And then, when Rachael was certain she would go crazy for wanting him, Dillon swept her legs apart and raised himself over her. "Guide me with your hand," he rasped against her parted lips. "Stop me if I hurt you."

Doing as he said, Rachael closed her hand around his hardness, guessing instinctively what she needed to do. She caressed the length of him, marveling at the smooth texture while guiding him to her. He prodded gently at the silken entry, hesitated, then thrust past the silent barrier in one fluid move. He paused at her quick intake of breath and the way her body stiffened.

"Are you okay?"

Rachael relaxed beneath his weight. "It feels . . . good."

That's all the encouragement he needed. Dillon sank fully against her softness and sighed his immense pleasure as the tiny muscles gripped him and held him captive. Carefully and gently, he moved against her, and after a moment, she, too, was caught up in the highly erotic dance. Their paces quickened—dipping, straining, pulling back, until finally, there was no holding back. They hung, suspended, then raced toward the white-hot sensations that waited to greet them. They were not disappointed.

Afterward, Rachael lay quietly in Dillon's arms, cozied up against his solid warmth, and she listened to his steady breathing that told her he had drifted off to sleep. For her, sleep was impossible.

She was simply too wound up, too happy, too much in love. She had never felt closer to another human being. She gazed up at him and thought he had never looked more handsome as he did now in sleep.

For the first time in her life, Rachael felt beautiful. In Dillon's arms, she had found the desire and passion she'd always yearned for. In his arms, she felt truly accepted, and it was easy to forget the bitter rejection she had suffered, and the insecurities that plagued her still. Dillon's strength and warmth sustained her and took the bite out of the grief she still felt over her father's death.

In Dillon's arms, she felt rejuvenated and hopeful. Rachael was certain there wasn't anything she couldn't do.

When Rachael opened her eyes the following morning, she found Dillon watching her, lying on his side, one arm tucked beneath his pillow. "Good morning, pretty lady," he said.

She blinked. "How long have you been awake?" How long had he been watching her, she really wanted to know, feeling very self-conscious at the thought.

He shrugged. "Half hour or so. Has anyone ever told you you're pretty in the morning?"

Rachael, gazing at him from her own pillow smiled softly and shook her head. "I don't often wake up with a man in my bed." She was thankful now that she had put her gown on after they had made love for the second time the night before. She yawned. "Why didn't you wake me?" she asked sleepily, noting the growth of beard on his jaw that made him appear devilishly handsome in the dim light.

"I was enjoying watching you sleep." He reached over and brushed a strand of hair from her cheek, and his expression softened. "Are you sore this morning?"

She blushed. "Not too bad."

"You should probably soak in a hot tub for an hour or so."

She laughed. "An hour or so? And be late serving your breakfast?" Her eyes automatically sought out the alarm clock as she spoke, remembering suddenly that she had forgotten to set it. She bolted upright on the bed when she saw how late it was. "Oh my," she said, reaching for her wrap. "Look at the time. Mr. Coot is probably on his way over right now for breakfast."

Dillon chuckled and reached for her. "Relax, Rachael. Coot is going to be preparing his meals in the bunkhouse for a couple of days. At his own insistence," Dillon added when she looked as though she might protest. "And you and I are taking the day off. Now, be a good wife and get over here next to me." He pulled her onto the bed once more.

Rachael went to him. He was naked beneath the covers, but once she got past her initial shyness, she relaxed in his arms, enjoying the feel of his big, hair-roughened body against hers.

And then before she knew it, she too was naked, and the hot bath was forgotten as she snuggled against Dillon. His chest hair chafed her breasts, and her nipples puckered in response. Kissing her deeply, Dillon toyed with her nipples until they peaked, hard and quivering. He broke the kiss.

"Touch me, Rachael," he said. She did as she

was told, laying her hand flat against his wide chest where she found his heartbeat. He chuckled, and she felt the rumbling sound against her open palm. "Not there, silly woman," he said, catching her hand in his. He moved it between his thighs, closing her palm around his hardness. "Here," he said.

Rachael blushed. "I'm going to need time to get the hang of this," she confessed.

The smile he offered her was brazen. "You can practice on me anytime." He closed his eyes and gave in to the sensations her unpracticed touch evoked. Heat flared in his loins. Finally, he swept the covers aside, grinning wickedly at his wife's shriek of protest.

"No, Rachael," he said firmly, when she made a wild grab for the bed sheet. "You're my wife now. No cowering beneath the covers, no locked doors, no undressing in the dark." He smacked her playfully on the behind. "You got that?"

The lovemaking that followed was slow and thorough, Dillon seeking out every curve and hollow of her body with his hands and lips. "Wrap your legs around my waist," he said once he'd sunk into her. She did so, and he groaned aloud, realizing his dreams of her doing that very thing had not come close to being as wonderful as the reality. He waited until he heard her gasp of delight before taking his own pleasure. "I'm crazy about you, Rachael McKenzie," he said once he'd floated back to earth.

Crazy about her? Rachael thought as he held her firmly against his chest afterward. Her brows furrowed into a small frown. She relaxed after a moment. Oh well, it wasn't love, but it was a good place to start.

After a while, Dillon dozed. Rachael quietly donned her wrap, slipped from the bed, and tip-toed out of the room. In the bathroom, she filled the old-fashioned bathtub with hot water and added a generous amount of bath salts. She sighed her immense pleasure as she sank fully into the steaming water and let it caress her sore muscles, muscles that her husband had so lov-ingly fondled only moments before. She thought about what he'd told her.

I'm crazy about you, Rachael McKenzie.

Rachael smiled, leaned back against the tub, and closed her eyes. It would do for now.

Suddenly the bathroom door was thrown open with enough force to make her jump. Rachael grabbed the sides of the tub to keep from sliding into the water, and she swung her head around in alarmed surprise.

Dillon stood there, his wide shoulders spanning the doorway, looking totally unabashed in his nakedness. He grinned as Rachael tried to cover herself from breast to thigh with a washcloth. "Scoot over," he ordered. "I'm coming in."

Once Dillon and Rachael had eaten a breakfast of blueberry pancakes that he had made from scratch in an old waffle iron that had belonged to Abel's wife, he suggested they take a walk. Dressed in thick sweaters, they started down the long driveway, holding hands. Dillon told Rachael about the early days on the ranch, trying to get along with Abel Pratt when nobody else could, and of the years he'd spent drifting.

"I guess that's why I was so determined to get

along with Abel," he said reflectively. "I was just sick and tired of always being on the move."

"Why did you leave home at such an early age?" she asked.

Dillon hesitated only a second before he answered. "I didn't get along with my old man," he told her. "I figured I could do better on my own." He paused and gazed toward a group of heifers and their calves grazing in the pasture. "We weren't what you'd call a typical family. There wasn't much stability or security growing up in a place where the main breadwinner stayed drunk much of the time. My parents were always fighting and yelling and carrying on as if they hated each other. I never knew what to expect from one day to the next." He shrugged. "My mother tried. She took us all to church now and then, but—" He pondered it. "I think she just got tired. I don't remember a time when she wasn't pregnant. After a while, she stopped caring about things. About the kids, the house, everything. She let him pull her down with him."

Rachael felt sad for him. "What are they doing now?"

"They're still together. Still fighting and yelling, because it's all they've ever known, I guess." He gave a derisive laugh. "And now my mother doesn't understand why I don't visit."

Rachael squeezed his hand. "I'm glad you told me that," she said. And she was. Already she was beginning to understand her husband better.

The following days were idyllic. Rachael awoke each morning in Dillon's arms after a night of lovemaking that left them totally spent but closer emotionally. Sometimes Dillon woke her in the wee morning hours and, despite her sleepy protests, Rachael found herself responding ardently and passionately to his lovemaking. Had anyone ever accused her of being a passionate woman, Rachael would have laughed in their face, but with Dillon, her passion flared to heights that both surprised and delighted her and made her giddy with love for him. Sometimes Dillon would wake her during the last dark hour before sunrise, and they would make love or simply talk until the sky changed into a soft mauve.

Rachael talked of her own childhood, a childhood that was vastly different from his, and he grew to respect the man who'd raised her with so much love and nurturing. He knew in his heart if he and Rachael were ever to have children, he would want to build that kind of closeness with them.

One afternoon, Rachael slipped into the bathroom where Dillon was showering, shrugged out of her clothes and stepped behind the shower curtain where he stood beneath the spray. Surprised his modest wife would act so boldly, Dillon greeted her warmly, pulling her tight against him.

He smelled like the outdoors, Rachael thought, nuzzling her face against his chest where the black hair glistened. She teased one brown nipple with her teeth and watched in fascination as it grew erect. She had enjoyed discovering his body since their wedding night, familiarizing herself with his scent, the textures. She never tired of touching him or watching him, whether he be standing at the bathroom sink shaving or brushing his teeth or sipping coffee at the kitchen table in the evenings while working on his ledgers.

She enjoyed learning his likes and dislikes, discovering his favorite desserts. She selected his favorite pies, apple and cherry, from the frozen-food section at the grocery store, baked them at home, then wrapped them in aluminum foil. And although Dillon got a kick out of it, he never teased her. But it warmed his heart to come into the house at the end of the day to the aroma of freshly baked pie.

Now Rachael nibbled his shoulder playfully and tasted the salt of his sweat, and she delighted in that as much as she had in everything else about him. Finally, in an act that was more brazen than anything she'd ever done, she lowered her hands between his thighs and caressed him until he filled her palm with his hardness. Dillon wasted no time doing the same, fingering the silken folds between her thighs until her legs trembled and her breathing quickened. He lifted her easily, positioning her legs around his waist, and he lowered her onto the length of him. Heat met heat, coiling so tightly in their bellies, they could only cling together and enjoy the burn. Their sighs rose and mingled with the warm spray from the shower as they shuddered in each other's arms. Dillon realized he had never felt closer to another human being in his life.

Rachael sensed a change in Dillon over the ensuing days, a softening of sorts, his features becoming more relaxed. He smiled more and complained less about her cooking and the fact that her church business kept her behind in her chores. She worked double-time to catch up on them so she could share the sofa in front of the television with Dillon in the evenings and work on her sermon. Coot usually stayed for an hour after dinner, at least until dessert, then excused himself as though sensing the two needed time alone. And even though Rachael often commented that Coot needed a wife, Dillon was quick to point out his friend had tried marriage three times and preferred being alone now.

If Rachael was pleased with Dillon's softening attitude, there were other things about him that bothered her. He still refused to go to church. Although her little congregation was growing bit by bit, her husband was not part of it. Two Sundays had passed with no Dillon, and Rachael was beside herself as to what to do. So she prayed and worried.

Not only did Dillon not attend church, he often forgot to shave in the mornings. And although he kept his promise about not going to the Mustang, he spent his Friday and Saturday nights playing cards in the bunkhouse with Coot until all hours, while Rachael practiced her sermon in front of the bathroom mirror. And when he climbed into bed sometime later, Rachael would pretend to be asleep, simply because it hurt to think he preferred Coot's company to hers. Didn't he spend enough time with Coot Jenkins? she wanted to ask him. Hurt quickly turned to resentment. She had changed in so many ways since their marriage, she told herself, trying to overcome her sense of modesty, trying to meet Dillon's emotional needs each time he opened up to her. But Dillon hadn't changed one iota where it mattered. Not once had he told her he loved her. Sometimes she felt she was so desperate to hear those three words that she wouldn't have cared if he meant them or not. He had freely admitted saying them to other women, yet not once had he said them to her. It hurt to think that she, who'd loved him best, could not evoke the same emotion from him.

Dillon came into the house one rainy Saturday night, only three weeks after the wedding, and hurried up the stairs to the bedroom, only to find it locked. He frowned and tried the doorknob again. "Rachael?" he called out. "Rachael, wake up, the door's locked."

The door was snatched open with such force that Dillon stepped back in surprise. "Darn right it's locked, Dillon McKenzie," she all but shouted, taking in his damp hair and clothes. "Do you have any idea what time it is?" When Dillon checked his watch, she stomped her foot impatiently. "It's one o'clock in the morning, that's what!"

Dillon was so stunned, he didn't know what to say. He raked his fingers through his hair and shrugged. "I guess I just lost track, that's all. I was only out in the bunkhouse with Coot."

"That's right, out in the bunkhouse with Coot. You're *always* in the bunkhouse with Coot."

"I'm not *always* in the bunkhouse with Coot," he said. "I drop in a couple of times a week. What's the big deal?"

"Three times this week," she accused.

"He's my best friend."

"And what am I?"

"You're my wife," he said, growing irritated with her now. "And I'm with you plenty. But if you think I'm going to ignore the best friend I've ever had just because you've got a possessive streak in you—"

"Possessive!"

"That's right. You act as if I'm supposed to spend every waking moment with you."

"I most certainly do not!"

"I don't go to the Mustang anymore," he pointed out.

"That was as much your decision as mine."

"Yeah, right."

Her anger flared at his sarcasm. "What's that supposed to mean?"

"It means I don't mind making a few concessions, but I'm not going to change my whole life for you. That wasn't part of the agreement."

"Agreement!"

"That's right. We agreed to become husband and wife, but you didn't saying anything about me going to church and giving up everything I like. Suppose I told you to give up your preaching."

"That's different and you know it."

"Not when it takes time away from our marriage, it isn't. You expect me to be at your beck and call, but if you're out visiting someone in the evening or on the telephone discussing someone's personal problems with them, I'm supposed to sit tight until you're finished."

"You knew I was a minister when you married me."

"And you knew what kind of man I was."

Rachael was about to answer but was interrupted when the telephone on her bedside table blared. Who could that be at this hour, she wondered. She hurried over to the phone and answered it.

From the doorway, Dillon listened and tried to make sense of what was going on. When she hung up, she was visibly shaken.

"What is it?" he asked, stepping into the room.

"That was Ellen Holden," Rachael told him, already moving to her closet. "There was an accident on the main highway. Dan was involved."

"Is he hurt?"

Rachael nodded as she opened her closet door and pulled out a skirt and sweater. "Several people were, but Dan lost a lot of blood. Ellen asked me to call around for donors."

"Then why are you getting dressed?" he asked.

"Because as soon as I make the calls, I'm going to the hospital myself. My blood type matches Dan's exactly."

"Did Ellen say what Dan was doing out on the highway at this hour?" Dillon asked, already knowing what her answer would be.

Rachael turned her back on him and pulled her gown over her head, then quickly reached for a bra. Although Dillon had seen her without clothes, she still felt funny undressing in front of him, and he imagined she always would. "He was coming home from the Mustang."

"He was drunk," Dillon said. "He always has too much to drink, then refuses to let anyone drive him home." When Rachael didn't respond, he went on. "Doesn't that bother you? I mean, you're against drinking, but you'll drive thirty miles in the rain to give blood to a man who makes a practice of it."

"It doesn't matter whether I believe in his lifestyle, I'm still obligated to help." She stepped into her skirt and zipped it.

"Why, Rachael? Why are you obligated?"

Rachael faced him, and for a moment she looked as though she might cry. "Because there are too many people in this world who don't care what happens to others, Dillon, and I'm not going to be one of them. I can't turn my back on another person's pain and suffering. Perhaps it's because I was raised that way. My father, with as many health problems as he had when he got older, thought nothing about climbing out of bed in the middle of the night to help someone."

"I'm not the man your father was, Rachael, and if you try to make me into him, you're going to be disappointed."

Rachael buttoned her blouse quickly. It had never occurred to her that she might be trying to do that. "Look, I really don't have time to discuss this, Dillon," she said. "I have to make my phone calls and go. Maybe we can talk tomorrow when I get back."

Dillon raked his fingers through his hair. "I'm not letting you drive to Harley in this weather. Make your calls. That'll give me time to dress and make a pot of coffee."

"That's not necessary."

"It is as far as I'm concerned."

The scene at the hospital was one of pandemonium when they arrived, the families of the accident victims having come as soon as they'd heard. Rachael was thankful to see that most of the people she'd called for blood had arrived as well, including Reverend Bartlett, the minister from the church in Harley who'd married her and Dillon only weeks before. He had contacted members of his congregation and asked for blood donations as well.

When it was Rachael's turn to go into the small lab and give blood, she hurried in. The nurse welcomed her warmly and helped her onto the table. "I'm a member of the church in Harley," she said. "Reverend Bartlett told us there was a new lady minister in Jasper and that she'd recently married one of the ranchers." The nurse inserted a needle in a vein in Rachael's arm. "I hope you'll be very happy, Reverend."

Rachael returned the smile. "Thank you."

Once she'd drawn the blood, the nurse told Rachael to continue lying there. "You know the routine," she said, "since you've obviously given blood a lot." She carried the pint-size container of blood to the next room and busied herself for a moment. "You can get up now," she told Rachael a few minutes later.

Rachael nodded and raised up from the table. The nurse helped her down while talking nonstop about all that had occurred at the hospital since the accident victims had come in. All at once, Rachael felt light-headed. "Wait—" She grasped the nurse's arm as the room pitched to one side.

"Is anything wrong, Reverend?"

Rachael promptly fainted.

"What the hell do you mean my wife passed out!" Dillon demanded of the nurse. "Did you take more blood out of her than you were supposed to?"

"Mr. McKenzie, *please!*" The nurse tried to quiet him. "There are enough upset people at this hospital as it is. You're only making matters worse."

"Where is she?" he asked, already stalking toward the lab.

Ellen Holden stopped him. "Dillon McKenzie, don't you dare go in there and upset Rachael," she said, using the same tone he'd heard her use on her children when they got into trouble. "Can't you see she's taking Dan's accident as badly as I am?

The poor girl just got dizzy. It's not unusual when people give blood."

Dillon halted. Ellen's eyes were red and swollen from crying, and he felt bad for causing such a ruckus when they didn't know if Dan was going to pull through or not. "I'm sorry, Ellen, it's just . . . Don't you think Rachael is too thin to give that much blood?"

Ellen pursed her lips. "Rachael is a lot stronger than you think, Dillon. And she's not that thin. Most women would give their right arm to have Rachael's figure."

Dillon felt very foolish. "I'm sorry for yelling at you," he told the nurse. "Could I see my wife now?"

The nurse nodded and smiled as though she were used to dealing with irrational husbands all the time. "Of course, Mr. McKenzie."

Dillon thought Rachael looked very pale when he found her lying on the table. "Are you okay?" he asked, coming up quickly beside her. He took one of her hands in his own and squeezed it.

Rachael nodded. "I'm fine, Dillon, really," she said. "I just got a little woozy, that's all."

"I thought you told me you had given blood plenty of times before."

"I have," she insisted, then repeated the same spiel she'd given the nurse. "I think I'm just run-down. I haven't felt like my old self lately." She turned her head slightly as her eyes filled with tears. She had never been one to cry easily but lately she felt like crying much of the time, crying over the fact she didn't have much of a congregation and over the problems in her marriage.

"Most of it is your own fault, Rachael," Dillon said. "You spend all day running up and down the road visiting people, then come home and try to stuff six hours of chores into two. It would wear anybody down." He paused. "Maybe Coot and I should help out more around the house," he grumbled after a moment.

"Mr. McKenzie, why don't you let your wife rest for a few minutes," the nurse suggested when she came back into the room. "Perhaps you wouldn't mind running to the cafeteria for some more juice. That always helps." Dillon reluctantly agreed to leave her.

"Feeling better?" the nurse asked Rachael.

Rachael nodded, feeling silly that she'd caused such a commotion with everything else that was going on. She'd never had a problem giving blood before. Perhaps it was because she was so worried about Dan and the others. "Much better. Thank you."

The nurse hesitated a moment before she spoke. "I hope you don't mind, Reverend, but I took the liberty of testing your blood while your husband was in here and—"

"Is something wrong?" Rachael looked slightly alarmed.

The nurse smiled. "Not unless you were planning to hold off on starting your family," she said. "You're pregnant, Mrs. McKenzie."

Ten

By morning, Dan Holden's condition had become stable. The other two men involved in the accident had suffered only minor injuries and were scheduled for release in a couple of days. Ellen Holden, who hadn't closed her eyes all night, sank against her chair in relief when the doctor told her he had every reason to be optimistic about Dan's condition.

"It was a pretty serious head injury, Mrs. Holden," he said, "but the tests don't indicate brain damage."

Rachael knew that Ellen had worried about that more than anything. What would she do with a brain-damaged husband and six children to support, she had whispered to Rachael more than once during the long night. And Rachael had taken her into the chapel to pray. And while she had prayed for Dan and Ellen and their family, she had prayed for Dillon and herself and the unborn child she now carried. And she wondered how Dillon would take the news. Did he really see her as a possessive woman who wanted to keep him away from everything he enjoyed? she wondered. Did he miss his friends at the Mustang, his old way of life? Would he come to resent her and even the baby as time passed?

"Why don't you go home and rest," Rachael told Ellen. "I'm sure your mother won't mind staying with the children today so you can catch up on your sleep."

Ellen reluctantly agreed to go. "I need to ask a favor of you, Reverend," she told Rachael before she left. Dillon, standing at a respectful distance, listened.

Rachael had never felt so weary in her life, but as she gazed into Ellen's swollen eyes, she knew there wasn't anything she wouldn't do to help the woman. She would have to put her own problems aside for the time being. "What is it, Ellen?"

"I want you to talk to Dan for me when he's better," she said, then paused as though slightly embarrassed to have to bring it up. "This isn't the first time something like this has happened." Her eyes filled with tears. "But this time he could have died."

Rachael's heart went out to the woman. "I'll talk to him, but I'm not sure it'll do any good."

"I want you to tell him I can't go on living like this," Ellen insisted. "I've got six kids who need a father. If he won't change, then I'm going to have to make some pretty painful decisions about my marriage." She wiped her eyes. "I don't know if I'm strong enough."

"You're stronger than you think," Rachael assured her.

"I wouldn't ask you to do this for me if there was somebody else I could turn to, but Dan would never speak to me again if I got one of his friends involved. He respects you." She smiled through her tears. "He says you're the only preacher he's ever met who didn't look down your nose at him. I mean, I know you don't approve of drinking and all, but Dan's a good person and a good father."

Rachael met Dillon's gaze over Ellen's head. "It's not that I'm opposed to people having a good time, Ellen," she said gently. "I know people need to have a little fun in their lives and relax. But I never see the fun times that people have with their drink. This is the part I see." She spread her hands to indicate the waiting room where they sat. "I only see the part where people are killed or maimed for life in drunk-driving accidents or women and children who are abused because of it. I don't like anything that hurts people, no matter what it is." She paused. "I will talk to Dan. I will do whatever I can to help. But you may have to make some changes as well."

Finally, once Rachael had seen to Ellen's needs, she turned to Dillon. "Would you mind driving me back to the ranch now?" she asked. "If we hurry, I can make it just in time for services."

Dillon frowned. "You're not going to worry about church *today*, are you? Lord, Rachael, you haven't slept all night." He was still concerned that she had fainted.

She smiled tiredly. "I'll make my sermon short today, how's that?" Her look sobered. "But I have to go, Dillon, you know that." She would rest later. Now that there was a baby, she would have to take care not to overdo it.

Dillon didn't understand why, after an all-night vigil at the hospital, she felt she had to hold services. But he knew arguing was useless. For some reason, Rachael felt responsible for the world's problems. It didn't matter if her own needs weren't met or those of her husband. He realized then just how much he resented her work at times, simply because it took so much time away from him. He knew he was being selfish, but he couldn't help it. They were newlyweds. Surely they could have some time for themselves once in a while. It wasn't up to Rachael to single-handedly make the world a better place. He wondered how other ministers' families coped.

"I'll take you back," he said begrudgingly, "but only if you promise to rest after the service. I don't need a sick wife on my hands."

Rachael knew he was only worried about her falling behind on her cooking and chores. "Yes, Dillon," she said. "We don't want that."

When they arrived back at the ranch, they found the Coopers already there, standing in the driveway, talking to several of the cowboys who'd started attending the services after the branding. They had heard about Dan and questioned Rachael about it the moment she stepped out of Dillon's pickup truck.

Rachael filled them in on the details while they filed in through the front door of the house. "I'm afraid I didn't get a chance to set the chairs out," she said as they crowded into the front room. "But those of you who can't find a seat, I would appreciate it if you'd just stand. The service is going to be short today."

Dillon, standing inside the front door, found himself answering questions about the accident as well and stepped aside as Coot hurried in looking embarrassed that he had overslept. Coot closed the door and leaned against it since there was no place to sit, but the move blocked Dillon's exit. And Rachael, who was tired and concerned only about getting started, immediately asked everyone to bow their heads and pray for Dan and the other accident victims.

Thus, it was by pure accident that Dillon McKenzie found himself attending church services for the first time in more than twenty years.

One morning the following week, Rachael announced her plans to go to Harley and meet with a builder. Dillon didn't quite meet her gaze. It was no secret that he didn't approve of spending the money on a new church, but he knew his hands were tied on the subject. Abel Pratt had allocated the money to her for such a purpose without considering what it might do to the ranch, and there was not a damn thing he could do about it. But then Dillon realized his hands were tied on a lot of issues concerning his wife and her vocation. She had made it clear from the beginning that her church work came first. It didn't make it any easier for him to accept, though. But instead of saying anything, Dillon scooted his chair from the table, telling Coot it was time to get to work.

Rachael stopped him before he went out the door. "I imagine I'll be gone most of the day," she said, "since I plan to go by and speak with Dan at the hospital. There's cold chicken and potato salad in the refrigerator for lunch." She saw that he wasn't pleased. "I'll try to be home in time for dinner."

Dillon nodded and walked out the front door without even so much as a good-bye. When Coot joined him on the front porch, he demanded to know what was going on.

"She's been acting weird lately," Dillon told him. "Ever since Dan landed in the hospital."

"Well, I couldn't help but notice how strained things have been between the two of you lately."

Coot didn't know the half of it, Dillon wanted to tell him. Not only had he and Rachael stopped talking, they had stopped making love, a fact which deeply disturbed him since Rachael had eagerly welcomed his affections before they'd argued about how much time he spent with Coot. What did she expect from him? he wondered. Did she want him to give up all his friendships and spend every free minute with her? Did she expect him to become more actively involved in her church work? He knew she was going to be sorely disappointed if that was the case. He would never be the kind of man her father had been. He couldn't be something he wasn't.

"I'm not sure about a lot of things where Rachael and I are concerned," he told Coot. He glanced in the direction of the house. "I'm not sure I like it when my own wife has more time to spend with Dan Holden than me." It sounded feeble, but it summed up his feelings where his wife was concerned. He didn't like being second in her life.

"She's just doing her job, Dillon."

"That's not the only thing," he said. "She doesn't look happy to me. And she's always snapping my head off, telling me how I don't shave enough, how I constantly track mud in on *her* clean floor. I can't do a damn thing to please her."

"You know what it is, don't you?" When Dillon merely shook his head, Coot went on. "It's PMS, man. All women have it. I should know after three marriages."

Dillon pondered it. "Well, that would explain why

she cries so easily, I suppose. How much longer will it last?"

"It can go on for a week or more. Ten days even." Coot said.

Dillon shook his head. "I don't know, Coot. I don't think I can put up with it for two weeks."

"Yeah, but there's a secret to it," Coot offered conspiringly. "You see, while she's walking around acting like the wife from hell, you're going to do everything you can to make it nice for her. When she cries and tells you what a rotten human being you are, you're going to sit there and nod your head and agree with everything she's saying. And then when she eats you out of house and home, you're going to keep the food coming as fast as you can. Of course, once she's eaten everything, she'll ask you if you think she's fat." Coot paused. "Now, this is where a man can lose his life if he's not careful. You say, 'No, honey, you're not fat at all. You're beautiful and sexy, and I'm thankful I married you.'"

Dillon frowned. "Why should I do all that?"

Coot grinned. "Because when it's all over and she returns to normal, she's going to feel so guilty about how she treated you that she'll fall all over herself trying to please you. It'll be payoff time for sure. She'll fix your favorite meal and wait on you hand and foot and wear those see-through gowns at night, and you can cash in on all you've gone through for two weeks."

"No kidding?" Dillon felt almost hopeful.

The sun was setting when Rachael pulled off the highway and turned into the long drive leading to the ranch. She glanced at the digital clock on her dash and frowned, knowing Dillon would not be in a good mood when she arrived home. He would have already quit for the day and showered for dinner, and he would be none too happy when he discovered she hadn't been there to put a hot meal on the table. But then, nothing she did made him happy these days.

I'm not going to cry, she told herself when she felt the ever-present lump in her throat. She had done nothing but cry for days now, and she knew it had everything to do with her pregnancy, which she had confirmed for herself only a few days before with a drugstore test in the privacy of her bathroom. Of course, she had cried over that too. Not that she didn't want a baby. She couldn't think of anything more satisfying or rewarding than giving birth to Dillon's son or daughter. But why did it have to happen now? she wondered. Her marriage was so new, so fragile at the moment, and she and Dillon were so different. They needed time to work out their differences, strengthen the bonds of their love before bringing a child into their lives.

But it was too late to worry about that now, because she was already pregnant, and Dillon, who seemed to resent his changing lifestyle, would feel even more so with the added responsibility of a baby.

So she cried. She cried when she got up in the morning and saw the beautiful sunrise, and she cried each time she saw it disappear for the day. She cried when she was forced to do simple things like scramble eggs for breakfast because it always brought to mind how chickens had such a terrible lot in life, living in wire cages and existing only for the pleasure of man.

As if she didn't have enough to worry about, she

thought dully. She couldn't even control her marriage, what made her think she could offer hope to poor, suffering chickens? Her own husband obviously didn't love her, and he clung to his own side of the bed at night as though he couldn't stand the thought of touching her. How would he feel when she grew bigger with their child?

Her job wasn't making things any easier for the two of them, she knew. Dillon resented the time she spent away from the house, resented the fact she needed to spend money on a church. After meeting with a builder that afternoon and discovering how much it *would* cost to build even a modest church, she was as concerned about the money as he was. But how could Dillon expect her to pile people into their living room every Sunday, for heaven's sake? And what about the Sunday school she needed so desperately for the children? Ellen Holden would make a perfect Sunday school teacher, she had decided after watching her interact with her six children. And Dan, now that he'd decided to quit drinking and join AA, would need to occupy himself so he wouldn't be tempted to slide back into his old habits. Perhaps one day, when he pulled his own life together, he might consider sharing what he'd gone through with others in his predicament.

But that still left her husband out in the cold. Dillon McKenzie had no aspirations about becoming a church member, much less involving himself in a future program. Why couldn't Dillon understand how important her job was? she wondered, more heartsick over the problem than ever. Why couldn't he understand that the chores would always get done sooner or later and she would try to have his meals on the table when she could, but that her work simply had to come first?

Dillon would never understand, she knew, and he would continue to begrudge those things that took her away from the ranch or put more on his back. Once the baby came, it would only make matters worse.

She hadn't told Dillon about the baby simply because she didn't want to add more of a strain to their relationship. And if worse came to worse, and it looked as though her marriage was indeed going to fail, she didn't want to try and scrape it together for the sake of a child. She had seen too many couples remain in an unhealthy relationship for the sake of their children, and even though she didn't condone divorce, neither did she think it was right for some people to stay together when there was no hope. Perhaps she and Dillon weren't meant to be, she thought, and once again the tears came close to the surface.

She was just tired, Rachael told herself as she parked before the house a minute later. She had never known such tiredness, and sometimes she felt as though she could sleep for a week. Perhaps after dinner she'd take a hot bath and go to bed early.

Rachael tried to fix a smile on her face as she walked through the front door, but she'd barely stepped inside the house when she was assailed by the smell of food. The past couple of mornings she'd spent leaning over the toilet bowl and hoping that Dillon wouldn't discover her secret before she was ready to tell him. She tried to ignore it, and, taking a deep breath, walked into the kitchen. She found Dillon and Coot standing near the stove, each wearing a white apron. Sitting atop Dillon's dark head was a crumpled chef's hat. She couldn't imagine where he'd gotten it.

"Well, hello," Coot said the minute he saw her. He nudged Dillon, who turned around and smiled as well.

"Hello, Rachael," Dillon said. When she didn't answer right away, he cleared his throat. "Coot and I decided we would fix dinner tonight so—" He'd been about to say, *So you wouldn't have to, and because I know I get kind of crazy about you putting meals on the table and all.* But he didn't say it. Instead, he glanced toward the table and shrugged. "I hope you're hungry."

Rachael glanced toward the kitchen table, where a mountain of food waited—two kinds of meats, several bowls filled to the brim with steaming vegetables. She had never seen so much food in her life. Dillon had obviously been starved to death to want to prepare so much. Her heart sank. She couldn't do anything right. Not only was her husband keeping to himself at night, he was having to prepare his own meals. She had let him down. They had let each other down. Rachael shook her head, and her eyes filled with tears. "I can't eat," she said, and burst into tears. She hurried out of the room, leaving both men confused.

Two Sundays later, Dillon attended church on purpose, and Rachael was so flustered she could barely get through her sermon. She couldn't help but wonder if he'd done so merely for her benefit, despite the fact that he hadn't bothered to shave or wear the suit she'd bought him. He was cordial enough and had stopped complaining about her job and everything else, but he was more distant than ever, spending much of his free time with Coot.

"We have just been through a difficult time," Rachael said now, letting her gaze wander across the room to where Ellen and Dan Holden sat with their six children. She smiled tremulously, thinking of how difficult it had been for Dan, his head still bandaged, to leave the hospital the day before and attend the nearest AA meeting, and how anxious Ellen was for him. She thought about her own life and the fact that she and Dillon seemed to be drifting further apart. And she thought of the baby nestled deeply in her womb who may never know the benefit of being raised by both parents. It was becoming increasingly clear that she and Dillon had made a serious mistake by marrying.

"I know there have been times in my life that I didn't think I would find the strength to go on," she confessed, and saw Dillon frown from the back of the room. "So, today, I'd like to talk about where we go for that strength. I think I should title this sermon 'Hard Times,' because in our life we are going to have hard times."

Once the service was over, Dillon and the men stepped outside, and the women chatted with one another. Ellen sent her children to play on the front porch so she could tell Rachael about the progress Dan was making both emotionally and physically. The accident had left him with headaches, but the doctor felt they would disappear before long.

Rachael nodded as Ellen talked, but she was only half listening as her gaze wandered to the window. Dillon was standing beside several cowboys who'd started attending after the branding. She continued to watch for a moment in half interest, until she saw one of the cowboys raise something to his lips and drink. A silver flask caught the sun and winked at her. Rachael felt her heart turn to stone at the sight of it. Dan Holden stood only a few feet away from the man.

For a moment Rachael was at a loss as to what to do. Dan, she was certain, was so new to the AA program that he wouldn't mention it to the cowboy and ask him to put the flask away. But Dillon knew. Why wasn't he doing something?

Ellen made for the door and stepped out on the front porch where her children were playing. Rachael wanted to stop her. It was bad enough that Dan would have to overcome his desire for drink in other places, but why should he have to be plagued with it at church of all places?

"We'd better head home so I can get dinner started," Ellen said, taking her youngest by the hand.

Rachael tried to concentrate on what she was saying but couldn't. Cigarette smoke flowed from the crowd of men with the density of a prairie fire, and she wondered whether it would be a bad influence on the children playing nearby. Dillon himself was puffing his cigarette as though it might be his last. The men suddenly roared with laughter, and Rachael stiffened, certain someone had told a dirty joke, and she hoped that someone hadn't been her husband. The cowboy took another drink.

Ellen looked in the direction of the men, and her smile faded from her face the minute her eyes landed on the man with the flask. She went rigid all over. "I don't believe this!" she all but shrieked. "I can't believe what I'm seeing." A hush fell over the crowd of men, and they turned their heads in her direction.

Rachael stepped forward. Perhaps they were jumping to conclusions. "Ellen, wait—"

"No, Rachael, I'm not going to keep quiet. I don't have your wonderful sense of patience. I've been through a lot these past couple of weeks, and I'm near the end of my rope. I expected to come to church and find solace and strength, but instead, I find a bunch of rowdy cowboys drinking out front, and your husband the ringleader." Tears filled her eyes. "I'd suggest that before you try and help me and my husband get our house in order, you get *yours* in order!" She stalked away, leaving Rachael feeling very foolish.

"I'm telling you, Coot, I have *had* it. I'm tired of doing her chores and cooking my own food and sleeping on the edge of the bed, and when I finally make an attempt to go to church, look what happens."

Coot nodded sadly as he sipped a cup of coffee in the bunkhouse. He watched the rain beat against the window outside as it had for more than an hour now, during which time he had listened patiently as Dillon had ranted and raved about his marriage. "I know, Dillon," he said, "but you're going to have to sit down and talk to her. That's what marriage is all about."

"I'm tired of talking," Dillon said. "I'm going over there and tell her once and for all, she either shapes up, or she's outa here."

"You can't blame her for getting upset at that cowboy, now," Coot said. "She had no way of knowing he was drinking something his doctor had prescribed for a chest cold."

"The guy told her as soon as he realized what the stink was about," Dillon said. "The poor man doesn't even drink, for Pete's sake. Besides, even if he did, it's none of Rachael's business. She was sticking her nose where it didn't belong."

"She's been through a lot with the Holden family these two weeks," Coot pointed out. "You'll have to admit it looked pretty bad with that cowboy holding a flask and all. How was Rachael supposed to know it was medicine?"

"That's not the point, Cooter. Rachael has no right to tell people how to live their lives."

"She accepted the man's apology, for heaven's sake. What more could she do?" Coot sounded exasperated. "You're itching for a fight, Dillon, that's all. You've been spending too much time with me when you should be spending it with your wife. If you want to go over there and yell at her—"

"I'm not going to yell at her. I'm going to ship her back to Sioux Falls where she belongs, if she doesn't come to her senses." Dillon reached for his Stetson and plopped it on his head. "When I get finished with her, she's going to be begging for a second chance."

"I hope you know what you're doing," Coot said. "Something tells me Rachael isn't the type to back down if she thinks she's right."

"We'll see about that." Dillon slammed out of the house, leaving Coot sitting at the kitchen table. He walked toward the ranch house, cussing the rain for all it was worth. All it did anymore was rain, he thought. His boots slapped the mud, and he took pleasure knowing he wasn't even going to bother to wipe his feet before going into the house. If

Rachael said one word about it, he'd tell her what she could do with her clean floors.

Dillon rounded the house and came to an abrupt halt when he noticed Rachael's car wasn't in the driveway. He muttered another colorful string of curses and stomped into the house, taking mud and grime with him. She was probably at the Holden ranch sucking up to Ellen about the misunderstanding, he guessed. But when he got to the bedroom, he realized the situation was more serious. One look at the empty closets, and he knew. Rachael had left him. The knowledge that she would actually walk out on him hit with the force of a freight train.

Eleven

Ellen Holden was clearly upset to hear Rachael had left, when Dillon drove over to her house looking for his wife. "It's all my fault," she said, her eyes filling with tears. "I shouldn't have made such a fuss. Dan told me that cowboy wasn't drinking whiskey as soon as we got in the car to come home, but I was too embarrassed to get out and apologize. Besides, it was none of my business if the man had been drinking, but—" She paused and sniffed. "It's been a rough time for me and Dan. I tried to call Rachael and apologize as soon as I got home, but there was no answer."

When Dillon started to leave, she stopped him. "You're going to have to call the sheriff, Dillon. I don't like the idea of her driving on these wet roads in her condition."

Dillon's look went blank. "What condition?"

Ellen bit her bottom lip. "Oh, damn, you don't know. I can't believe you really don't know. You men are so thick-skulled sometimes that it amazes me."

Dillon was growing both agitated and angry. "Ellen, what the hell is it that I don't know?"

"Your wife is pregnant, Dillon."

The rain fell steadily, mixing with the ooze of oil and grime and puddling on the highway like melted butter. Rachael gritted her teeth when her car slid to one side, and she wished she were a cussing woman. She'd been driving for two hours now, going around in circles, actually, because she had no idea *where* she was going to go now that she had walked out on her husband and their marriage. Piled in the backseat was everything she owned.

She glanced in the mirror and frowned at the puffy red eyes that stared back at her. She hadn't stopped crying since she had left the ranch. No wonder she couldn't think straight, she told herself, and she wondered if she was crying because of her failed marriage or because pregnant women seemed to cry a lot, or both.

It wasn't going to look good for her, a minister, to have to file for a divorce, she thought. She spent all her time telling people how to pull their marriages together, but she had no inkling how to save her own. Perhaps she could have her marriage annulled, she thought hopefully.

Rachael gritted her teeth again. Why the heck should she worry about how things looked? Her life was falling apart, and she was worried about appearances. But that's how she'd always been. She had always had to consider each move carefully. Well, she couldn't continue to do that, she realized, because she was a human and made mistakes the same as everybody else. She hadn't been blessed with divine wisdom as some people thought.

She had fouled up in a big way by marrying Dillon McKenzie. What had ever made her think it would work? she wondered as fresh tears filled her eyes. She had acted irresponsibly, marrying him because she so desperately wanted those sparks in her life. She had married him knowing he didn't love her, thinking she could love him enough for the both of them. And she *had* loved him. She had yielded to him passionately in bed, thinking no woman had the right to be so happy and know such intense pleasure. But sometimes love was simply not enough. A man and woman had to have common goals, and hers and Dillon's didn't even come close.

She would have to return to Sioux Falls, she decided. She still had friends there, people who would see her through this bad time and support her decision to have a baby alone. She would sell her share of the ranch back to Dillon at a fair price and lay low until the baby came, then start anew, once her pain had subsided sufficiently. She was a strong woman. She had risen above the grief of her father's death, and she had recovered from the awful rejection of her old congregation, telling herself it had been their loss. It bothered her, too, that she had begun to get close to some of the people in Jasper, but had to walk away because of her crumbling marriage. Some of those people needed her, and she ached at the thought of not being able to help them.

But she knew in her heart it was nothing compared to the ache she suffered over Dillon McKenzie.

Rachael spotted the neon sign announcing the

Teddy Bear Motel and pulled off the road. As she parked near the office under the vacancy sign, she tried not to notice what a grungy place it was. She was simply too exhausted and distraught to care at the moment. She would rest for a while, then calmly plan her next move. If she was going to go back to Sioux Falls, she would not arrive looking beaten down, with her tail tucked between her legs. Nobody needed to know how badly her heart was breaking.

Night had fallen by the time Dillon received word from the Sheriff's Department that Rachael's car had been located in the parking lot of the Teddy Bear Motel outside of town. For hours he and Coot had paced the floor and stared out the window and tried not to think the worst. Dan and Ellen Holden had called several times with suggestions on how to find her.

"Do you know who any of her friends were in Sioux Falls?" Ellen had asked.

Dillon had had to tell her he didn't, and he realized sadly that he knew very little about his wife. He had been on his own for so long that he didn't know how to care about other people. When he expressed as much to Coot, the older man disagreed.

"You took care of Abel like he was your own father," Coot pointed out, "and you've always treated me very good. You can make it work between you and Rachael, if you want it bad enough."

And it surprised Dillon that he did want it to work. Once he'd gotten over his initial anger, he realized just how much he wanted her, just how much he cared for the minister with gorgeous blue eyes who'd taken over his life so completely. And when he thought of her in those white aprons, looking fresh and sweet, and how she'd felt in his arms each night, small and feminine and very sexy, his heart ached that he may not get a second chance with her. And now there was a baby. A baby!

He had not told Coot about the baby because he'd needed time to absorb the news himself. Already, he was wondering where they would put the nursery and thinking he would have to help Rachael more, stop making so many demands on her. The reason he insisted on her having hot meals on the table at a certain time, he knew, had little to do with being hungry but everything to do with the fact he'd never been able to count on it as a child. He liked the feeling of stability it represented, he liked knowing there were some things he could count on in life. But those feelings came from inside a man, he told himself now. He couldn't expect Rachael to fill needs that he was responsible for himself.

"I'm going to her," Dillon said after a moment, reaching for his Stetson. "She may not agree to come back to me, but it won't be because I didn't try."

Rachael bolted upright in the bed the minute the pounding started, her heart thundering in her chest from being awakened from a deep sleep. She blinked, trying to orient herself to her surroundings, and when she realized where she was, her heart felt heavy.

"Open up, Rachael, I know you're in there."

Dillon! Rachael scrambled off the bed. What was he doing there? How had he found her? She hurried to the door and checked to make sure it was locked. He knocked again.

"Go away, Dillon. I don't want to see you," she said. She had cried so hard for so long that her voice sounded funny.

On the other side of the door, Dillon sighed his frustration. "Rachael, please open the door. I have to talk to you." When she didn't answer, he cursed under his breath. "Rachael, we *are* going to talk," he insisted. "Now, you either open this door, or I'm going to get my tools out of the truck and take the damn thing off its hinges."

He was crazy enough to do it, she thought. Rachael unlocked the door, slid the chain free, and pulled it open. "You and I have nothing to say to each other, Dillon McKenzie," she said. "I'm leaving you. I'll sell my share of the ranch back to you, cheap, like you've wanted from the beginning, and then I'll be out of your hair forever." She started to close the door, but he blocked it with his boot and shoved it open with very little difficulty. He stepped into the room, his shoulders spanning the doorway, and the room seemed to shrink in size.

Dillon closed the door behind him and locked it, determined to say what he'd come to say. But when he faced his wife, he couldn't speak at first. She'd been crying again, and it tore at his gut to see her tear-swollen eyes. "I can get you out of my hair, Rachael," he said gently, "but how am I going to get you out from under my skin."

She hitched her head high. This was not what she had expected from him. "You don't love me, Dillon, so don't pretend otherwise."

He stepped closer. "You're wrong. I've loved you

from the beginning, but I was too stubborn to admit it. And I was scared. It's easy to tell a woman you love her when you don't really mean it, because you haven't invested yourself." He paused. "I was afraid if you knew how much I loved you that you would set about trying to change me. I couldn't risk that." This time he smiled. "You see, I might not be much, but I'm all I've had all these years. I didn't want to lose myself."

Rachael felt guilty as his words hit home. She *had* thought to change him. She had hoped to make him a better man, thinking it might somehow make her a better woman, a better minister. Perhaps she should have spent more time concentrating on his good qualities, she thought. Perhaps she should have applauded his attendance at church that day instead of noticing he hadn't shaved.

When Rachael didn't speak right away, Dillon went on. "I know I'm hardheaded and selfish, Rachael," he confessed, raking his hands through his damp hair. "But I've never really worried about anybody but myself. I left home young, and I've been on my own ever since. Now I'm tired of that kind of life. I like having someone next to me, somebody else to worry about, somebody to share my life with." He shook his head after a moment. "But I can't be all those things you want no matter how hard I try," he said. "I mean, I don't mind going to church on Sunday, but come Saturday night, I don't want to sit around and listen to your sermon when I know I'm going to hear it the next day too. I'd rather spend some time with Coot." He paused. "I'll try not to spend so much time with him in the future, though, because—" He gulped. "I know we need to spend more time together. I've known it all along, but I was trying to get back at you for being so involved in your church work."

Which brought them to a major problem in their marriage, she thought. "You resent my being a minister," she said. She walked over to the bed and sat down, gathering the blankets around her. She felt vulnerable with Dillon, always had.

"I don't resent the work, but I sometimes feel left out," he admitted. "You've told me numerous times how your church work is your top priority but . . ." He looked embarrassed. "Sometimes I need you too, Rachael. Not as one of your church members but as a man. Your husband. I want to feel equally important."

"You *are* important, Dillon," she said. She stood suddenly. "It probably wouldn't behoove me to have it known throughout my congregation, but you are as important to me as my work. If not more," she confessed. Maybe that's why she had worked so hard lately, because she'd suspected her love for Dillon was taking higher priority than everything else. But she could not help feeling that love any more than she could stop her heart from beating.

He was glad she had finally told him where he stood in her life. He wondered if she knew what it meant to him. "You can't expect everyone to live up to your standards," he said simply, remembering one of the problems that had led them to this point.

She nodded slowly. How many times had she told herself the same thing because of what had happened with the cowboy that afternoon. She only hoped he wouldn't let the misunderstanding keep him from coming back to church. "I realize that now, Dillon. I can't *tell* people how to live. I

can only be there for them when they need me."
She smiled self-consciously. "I sometimes have
trouble being objective because I get personally
involved."

"Is that what happened with me?" he asked.
When his question drew a blank look from her he
went on. "When I asked you to marry me, I told you
you'd be saving me from myself. But that's not
really what I wanted. I wanted you to marry me
because you loved me and wanted to spend the rest
of your life with me."

"I thought you knew that."

Dillon closed the distance between them and
gazed down at his wife, feeling his emotions swell
inside. He wanted to tell her how happy he was
about the baby, but he didn't, simply because he
didn't want her to think that was why he'd come
and why he was trying to pull their marriage back
together. He could trust Ellen Holden to keep her
tongue, he knew, and perhaps one day he would
admit it to Rachael, one day when she felt secure
enough with him. He was going to do everything in
his power to give her that security.

"Do you think you can overlook my faults,
Rachael?" he asked. "I'll never be the man your
father was, but can you find enough good in me to
make it worthwhile? Can you love me in spite of
my shortcomings?" When her eyes filled with
tears, he pulled her against him. "If you can do
that for me, I will promise to try and be the best
man I can." After a moment, he added with a
chuckle, "And overlook the way you cry all the
time."

Rachael laughed and swiped the tears with her
hand. "I can overlook your faults, if you can overlook mine," she said. He was good in the ways that
mattered, she knew.

Dillon kissed her then, delighting in the taste of her, sweetness blending with the salt of her tears. He pulled her tighter against him, feeling the need to hold her close so she never got away from him again. "I'll try to be more understanding in the future, Rachael," he promised.

"Dillon, about the church—"

He shook his head. "I don't want to talk about the church anymore, Rachael. I've complained about it long enough." He swallowed. "We're going to build the church you want."

Rachael felt her heart fill with love for the man who'd changed so much in spite of his determination not to. "I've decided to renovate the old schoolhouse," she said. "It will be cheaper, but I'll still have what I need. I can add on a room for the Sunday school classes, then as my congregation grows, I'll add more rooms." She paused. "Once I thought about it, it made perfect sense. And it seemed fitting that I should use the building where my father started preaching."

"Are you sure?"

She nodded. "You've accused me of having my head in the clouds, and perhaps you were right. But Abel's will wasn't completely fair, I'm afraid. This way, I can have my church, and you can have your tractor."

Dillon didn't know what to say. He was deeply touched that she would make the sacrifice. Nobody had ever cared enough for him to do such a thing. "I love you, Rachael," he said. "It feels good to say it and really mean it."

Rachael nuzzled her face against his chest, feeling intensely happy. She was thankful he had waited until he was certain before saying those three words. It had been worth the wait. She slipped her arms around his waist. "Let's stay here for the night, Dillon," she suggested shyly. "I know the place isn't much, but . . . I've missed you. I don't ever want you to sleep on the couch again."

Dillon gazed around the room and saw that it was indeed one of the tackiest motel rooms he'd ever been in. Rachael deserved better. She deserved a honeymoon in a posh hotel. But right now he couldn't think past wanting to hold her in his arms and make love to her and feel her quiver beneath him. "We can stay tonight, I suppose, but then I'm going to take you someplace decent for a few days. We need some time together, and I was selfish not to see it in the beginning. Maybe we'll get crazy and take a week," he added with a short laugh. "Maybe we'll go dancing. A woman as pretty as you deserves to be asked to dance."

Dillon pulled the blanket away and saw that she was dressed only in her slip. "But first, I want to make love to my wife." Without another word, he lifted her in his arms and carried her to the bed.

"There's something I need to tell you, Dillon," she said, as he lay her down gently and kissed one shoulder. She now felt confident enough to tell him about the baby. Surely there wasn't anything their love couldn't withstand.

"Later, Rachael." He pulled down the straps from her slip and marveled as he always did at the texture of her skin. "We have the rest of our lives." He knew then that no matter what life dished out he could handle it, overcome the obstacles. There would be no more drifting for him, no more running away. With Rachael at his side, he found hope. "We have forever," he added softly.

THE EDITOR'S CORNER

Come join the celebration next month as LOVESWEPT reaches an important milestone—the publication of LOVESWEPT #500! The journey has been exceptionally rewarding, and we're proud of each book we've brought you along the way. Our commitment to put the LOVESWEPT imprint only on the best romances is unwavering, and we invite you to share with us the trip to LOVESWEPT #1000. One step toward that goal is the lineup of six fabulous reading treasures we have in store for you.

Please give a rousing welcome to Linda Jenkins and her first LOVESWEPT, **TOO FAR TO FALL**, #498. Linda already has five published romances to her credit, and you'll soon see why we're absolutely thrilled to have her. **TOO FAR TO FALL** features one rugged hunk of a hero, but Trent Farraday is just too gorgeous for Miranda Hart's own good. His sexy grin makes her tingle to her toes when he appears at her door to fix a clogged drain. How can a woman who's driven to succeed be tempted by a rogue who believes in taking his time? With outrageous tenderness, Trent breaches Miranda's defenses and makes her taste the fire in his embrace. Don't miss this wonderful romance by one of our New Faces of '91!

In **THE LADY IN RED**, LOVESWEPT #499, Fayrene Preston proves why that color has always symbolized love and passion. Reporter Cassidy Stuart is clad in a slinky red-sequined sheath when she invades Zach Bennett's sanctuary, and the intriguing package ignites his desire. Only his addictive kisses make Cassidy confess that she's investigating the story about his immensely successful toy company being under attack. Zach welcomes the lovely sleuth into his office and as they try to uncover who's determined to betray him, he sets out on a thrilling seduction of Cassidy's guarded heart. As always, Fayrene Preston writes with spellbinding sensuality, and the wonderful combination of mystery and romance makes this book a keeper.

Glenna McReynolds sets the stage for an enchanting and poignant tale with **MOONLIGHT AND SHADOWS**, LOVESWEPT #500. Jack Hudson blames the harvest moon for driving him crazy enough to draw Lila Singer into his arms the night they meet and to kiss her breathless! He has no idea the beautiful young widow has relinquished her dreams of love. Lila knows there could only be this sensual heat between them—they have nothing else in common. Jack has never backed down from a challenge, and convincing Lila to take a chance on more than one special night together is the sweetest dare of all. A beautiful love story that you won't be able to put down.

Guaranteed to heat your blood is **THE SECRET LIFE OF ELIZABETH McCADE**, LOVESWEPT #501 by Peggy Webb. Black Hawk burns with the same restless fever that Elizabeth McCade keeps a secret, and when this legendary Chickasaw leader hides from his enemies in her house, he bewitches her senses and makes her promise to keep him safe. But nothing can protect her from the uncontrollable desire that flares between them. Elizabeth is haunted by painful memories, while Hawk has his own dark shadows to face, and both must overcome fears before they can surrender to ecstasy. Together these two create a blazing inferno of passion that could melt the polar ice caps!

Marvelous talent Laura Taylor joins our fold with the sensational **STARFIRE**, LOVESWEPT #502. With his irresistible looks, business superstar Jake Stratton is every woman's fantasy, but professor Libby Kincaid doesn't want to be his liaison during his visiting lecturer series—even though his casual touch makes her ache with a hunger she can't name. Jake's intrigued by this vulnerable beauty who dresses in shapeless clothes and wears her silky hair in a tight bun. But Libby doesn't want to want any man, and capturing her may be the toughest maneuver of Jake's life. A real winner from another one of our fabulous New Faces of '91!

Finally, from the magical pen of Deborah Smith, we have **HEART OF THE DRAGON**, LOVESWEPT #503. Set in exotic Thailand, this fabulous love story features Kash Santelli—remember him from *The Silver Fox and the Red Hot Dove*? Kash is prepared to frighten Rebecca Brown off, believing she's a greedy schemer out to defraud her half sister, but once he meets her, nothing about the minister's daughter suggests deception. Indeed, her feisty spirit and alluring innocence make him want to possess her. When Rebecca finds herself in the middle of a feud, Kash must help—and Rebecca is stunned by her reckless desire for this powerful, enigmatic man. Riveting, captivating—everything you've come to expect from Deborah Smith . . . and more.

And (as if this weren't enough!) be sure to look for the four spectacular novels coming your way from FANFARE, where you'll find only the best in women's fiction. **REAP THE WIND** by bestselling author Iris Johansen is the thrilling conclusion to the

unforgettable Wind Dancer trilogy. **THE SWANSEA DES-
TINY** by much-loved Fayrene Preston is the long-awaited prequel
to her SwanSea series from LOVESWEPT. Critically acclaimed
Virginia Lynn delivers another humorous and exciting Wild West
historical in **CUTTER'S WOMAN,** and Pamela Morsi follows
the success of her first book with **COURTING MISS HATTIE,**
a very touching story of a spinster who finds true love.

What a terrific month of reading in store for you from LOVESWEPT
and FANFARE!

With warmest wishes,

Nita Taublib

Nita Taublib
Associate Publisher, LOVESWEPT
Publishing Associate, FANFARE
Bantam Books
666 Fifth Avenue
New York, NY 10103

FANFARE

Enter the marvelous new world of Fanfare!
From sweeping historicals set around the globe to
contemporary novels set in glamorous spots,
Fanfare means great reading.
Be sure to look for new **Fanfare** titles each month!

On Sale in August:
GENUINE LIES
By Nora Roberts
author of PUBLIC SECRETS

*In Hollywood, a lady learns fast: the bad can be beautiful,
and the truth can kill.*

FORBIDDEN
By Susan Johnson
author of SWEET LOVE, SURVIVE

*Daisy and the Duc flirt, fight, and ultimately flare up in
one of the hottest and most enthralling novels
Susan Johnson has ever written.*

BAD BILLY CULVER
By Judy Gill
author of SHARING SUNRISE

*A fabulous tale of sexual awakening, scandal, lies and a
love that can't be denied.*